REINIGEN

Creative Texts Publishers products are available at special discounts for bulk purchase for sale promotions, premiums, fund-raising, and educational needs. For details, write Creative Texts Publishers, PO Box 50, Barto, PA 19504, or visit www.creativetexts.com

Reinigen
by David McElhinny
Published by Creative Texts Publishers
PO Box 50
Barto, PA 19504
www.creativetexts.com

ISBN: 978-1647380786

REINIGEN

by David McElhinny

CREATIVE TEXTS PUBLISHERS

Barto, PA

Thank you to Ms. Barbara Cimador, a teacher who went above and beyond to help her students succeed. My sophomore year of high school she believed in me, gave me confidence and is directly responsible for my 30-year career as a writer.

TABLE OF CONTENTS

CHAPTER ONE 1
CHAPTER TWO 4
CHAPTER THREE 7
CHAPTER FOUR 13
CHAPTER FIVE 16
CHAPTER SIX 23
CHAPTER SEVEN 29
CHAPTER EIGHT 36
CHAPTER NINE 41
CHAPTER TEN 45
CHAPTER ELEVEN 48
CHAPTER TWELVE 53
CHAPTER THIRTEEN 57
CHAPTER FOURTEEN 61
CHAPTER FIFTEEN 65
CHAPTER SIXTEEN 68
CHAPTER SEVENTEEN 72
CHAPTER EIGHTEEN 78
CHAPTER NINETEEN 83
CHAPTER TWENTY 86
CHAPTER TWENTY-ONE 90
CHAPTER TWENTY-TWO 97
CHAPTER TWENTY-THREE 101
CHAPTER TWENTY-FOUR 104

CHAPTER TWENTY-FIVE 110
CHAPTER TWENTY-SIX..... 115
CHAPTER TWENTY-SEVEN 118
CHAPTER TWENTY-EIGHT..... 123
CHAPTER TWENTY-NINE 126
CHAPTER THIRTY 133
CHAPTER THIRTY-ONE..... 142
CHAPTER THIRTY-TWO..... 146
CHAPTER THIRTY-THREE 151
CHAPTER THIRTY-FOUR..... 154
CHAPTER THIRTY-FIVE..... 157
CHAPTER THIRTY-SIX..... 160
CHAPTER THIRTY-SEVEN 163
CHAPTER THIRTY-EIGHT 169
CHAPTER THIRTY-NINE..... 174
CHAPTER FORTY 176
CHAPTER FORTY-ONE..... 189
CHAPTER FORTY-TWO..... 195
CHAPTER FORTY-THREE 202
CHAPTER FORTY-FOUR..... 212
ABOUT THE AUTHOR..... 215

CHAPTER ONE

Trudging along the frozen ground, the occasional tuft of long dead vegetation crunching beneath his boots, he walks with a slight forward lean, bracing himself against the constant, icy wind. Layered from head-to-toe in what were once high-quality clothes, now looking more like soot-stained rags, he presses on, head down, face covered, squinting against the penetrating conditions. A long, heavy, black coat gives him the look of a gunslinger, hiding much of his form, impossible to ascertain his true size or build. He carves his way through desolation that not long ago was vibrant and brimming with life.

Wisps of darkened snow dance and scamper along the barren Earth as he pushes forward. Even with his face covered, the stink of this decaying world penetrates the makeshift mask, his nostrils filled with the sulfur-filled scent that can best be described as the smell of death.

Some say he was recruited. Others say he was drafted. For a while, he felt like he was kidnapped. But none of it really matters. His life is certainly better than these few, remaining humans who live like cockroaches, desperately trying to make it through one more day.

These conditions have forced a psychological metamorphosis in him. He has become more than human, or is it less? He can't be sure. For the most part, he can put up that insulating mental shield, hardened to what he must do each and every day, but during stretches like this, when he has been alone for so long at one time, he begins to question his purpose. He knows he shouldn't, but sometimes when exposed to so much suffering and death for this long, even he, the most perfectly trained of soldiers, becomes emotionally compromised. But maybe that's a good thing, because it shows that, just maybe, he at least has some humanity left in him.

It has been six weeks this time, his longest excursion so far, but each time out he has less success than the time before as these brutal conditions are making the world less habitable by the day. For a time, there were factions that banned together, raiding other survivors to conquer, kill and take their resources. But as food and resources dried up and illnesses spread, even strong groups were eviscerated. These days, a group of five is considered large and one can walk for days without seeing another living person.

During the day, the heavy cloud cover and darkened skies allow just enough light to make visibility possible on this barren, gloomy rock that he calls home. While the sun is actually never in view, its faint light does creep through. But at night, pitch blackness makes it impossible to travel safely as anybody thoughtless enough to move around in the evening could easily walk right off the side of a cliff. Only a fool would use a lit torch as it would make any traveler an easy mark for those hiding in the shadows. At least an hour before total darkness engulfs the Earth, he always stops and finds some shelter. It's a routine that he has down to a science as he knows exactly what to look for and how to survive.

While his enhanced night vision allows him to see to some degree at night where others are blind, the bone-chilling temperatures make preparing a warm camp, with a strong shelter from the sky, imperative. On this night, an outcropping from the rocky terrain down deep in a valley will do nicely. It will provide cover from the constant wind and the indentation in the rocks is vital.

From his old, weathered, waterproof backpack, he removes a container full of water and takes a long, satisfying pull on it, quenching his thirst from a day of traveling. It contains a biofiltration system that allows him to use any water he finds, most of which is contaminated. He then removes a container full of sliced oranges, unscrews the lid and begins devouring the contents.

With daytime temperatures never getting above the 30s, the days are quite cold. But the nights are downright brutal as wind chill levels often reach negative numbers and without proper shelter, frostbite and death is imminent.

He removes a package from his backpack, carefully folded, opening a long, thin roll of material. He sets up the tiny tent, erecting it as far into the makeshift cave as possible and in less than two minutes, home for the evening is prepared. The tent is small and dark green in color, only two feet high, three feet wide and seven feet long. It looks kind of like a coffin when set up. He then wiggles his way into the tent, sealing the door behind him with heavy, Velcro straps. He then produces a small, black object made of durable plastic that is about the size of a brick. Checking the battery life, he sees that it is in the red now. Definitely in need of a charge, but enough juice for a few more days. He flicks it on and the coils inside spring to life with an orange glow. He hangs it from a small, fabric hook above him, and with a low hum, it begins already circulating heat.

In a matter of minutes, the heat from the device, reflected off the specially designed, insulated interior of the tent, makes the space warm and balmy. Soon he ends up shrugging off his jacket, then his shirt until he is bare-chested.

He lies on his back, folding his hands across his scarred torso, each healed wound a reminder of the life he leads. His beard has grown during his days in this wasteland, the laceration on his eyebrow just one week old is nearly gone thanks to his exaggerated healing and immune system function.

His light brown hair is nearly black from the grime of this world, and he feels as though he may never be clean again. It feels so good to shut his eyes and he rubs them hard with the heels of his thick, powerful hands, as if he is trying to erase the images he has seen. Then, in minutes, he drifts off to sleep.

His name is Mason.

CHAPTER TWO

Having carefully repacked his tent and secured his gear in the pre-dawn hours, Mason wants to make use of every bit of the daytime light in an effort to get home as soon as possible. While Mason's endurance is seemingly superhuman, even he is feeling the fatigue as the rigors of this journey is affecting him.

For several hours, he walks in a light, but constant, cold drizzle, seeing nothing and nobody. This is unfamiliar terrain for him as this is a new region he has been exploring. His hooded overcoat is waterproof, but the constant, penetrating rain is slowly creeping its way in just enough to be annoying. Finally, he comes along train tracks and begins following it east. He has found that people have a tendency to make camps along the tracks as travel is easier due to the fact that most of these routes are on relatively flat regions.

While walking is indeed easier, there is also an added element of danger as certain areas are perfect places for an ambush. Desperation has caused a terrifying change in what were once reasonable people. Therefore, anybody out here is capable of violence in an attempt to survive. For this reason, Mason stops often, scanning the horizon and listening intently for any sounds that trigger his heightened senses.

In what Mason guesses is early afternoon, the sky begins swirling and the clouds darken rapidly in the foreboding way that he has learned not to ignore. In this relatively open expanse, there are few places to find cover, so he begins double-timing it, the forty pounds of gear on his back making the effort all the more difficult. The gray clouds have now transformed into an inky black and what were distant rumbles of thunder have now become closer and are accompanied by random bolts of lightning. This storm is organizing quickly and time is of the essence. In a land with countless ways to die, these storms are one of the biggest threats.

In the distance, Mason sees a string of metal boxcars, badly dented and full of holes. While none have a roof, it is quite possible that some are being occupied, but he doesn't have the luxury of carefully surveying the area for danger. With the heavens now bellowing with fury this has the potential to be one of the bigger storms he has seen. Normally, one wouldn't seek cover in metal boxcars, but electricity is the lesser of the two dangers that these storms offer and with no other cover available, his choices are limited.

The first three cars are so badly damaged that they will offer no protection, but the fourth is mostly intact and he can even make out a Union Pacific logo on a partially intact wall. But Mason can feel that maximum cover will be required, so he opts to crawl under it, wiggly his way beneath the car, situating himself directly between the metal wheels where the suspension is the strongest. The whipping wind and thunder is soon accompanied by thumping echoes all around, occasionally shaking the entire line of boxcars, some of which are still hitched together after all this time, while others have been knocked over.

He was lucky to come across shelter when he did. With a storm of this magnitude, being caught out in the open could have been a death sentence and he would have been just another of the billions of corpses that are now scattered across the world. Mason has been surrounded by death for so long that he is numb to it now. In fact, he isn't even afraid of it. He is sure that normal people fear the prospect of their lives ending, but he doesn't. He will do whatever it takes to survive, but that's due to his training, not some imbedded genome that craves to live. He's basically programmed and that is something he dislikes about himself. As the storm intensifies, he realizes that philosophizing about what makes him tick is not an efficient use of his time and resources, so he shuts it off.

The onslaught continues for quite a while, but Mason is unsure of how long because he long ago learned that a soldier must be able to take advantage of any and all opportunities to rest. Therefore, using meditation techniques that he has mastered over the years, he uses his pack as a pillow, crosses his boots at the ankles, rests his hands on his chest, and actually drifts off to sleep while the region is pulverized from the sky.

While he is able to tell his mind to ignore the sounds of the storm, when it eventually subsides and he hears a gentle knocking on one of the metal doors further down the track, he is immediately awake and alert. It's that ability to selectively hear dangerous sounds while sleeping that has kept him alive. With the storm now over, he decides to leave his pack under the box car and investigate. Perhaps it is somebody trapped. Or maybe somebody is signaling others. But as the clanging continues in an erratic manner, Mason begins to suspect that no real danger exists. He slides out from his hiding spot, moving along the track, zeroing in on the sound. His senses alert for danger, he lets his defenses down when he discovers the noise. The storm knocked what was left of a sliding door on one of the boxcars off the track where it dangles against the side, the wind slowly causing it to clang off the frame.

After doing a thorough inspection of the 30-plus cars, most of which are just shells that have been battered nearly beyond recognition, he discovers that the entire area is indeed abandoned. The storm forced him to halt his journey for several hours and now it is late in the day. While he had hoped to be many miles further down the track by now, he knows that darkness will be upon him soon. So, he makes his way back to his pack and sets up camp, including his tent, right under the railcar for the night. He will just have to wait a little while longer to get home.

CHAPTER THREE

A dirty black snow highlights his morning commute, an ominous-looking sky offering the threat of another storm. The natural environment has been violated to the point where conditions are volatile and full of ever-changing violent outbursts. Mason makes an ongoing mental catalog of places to seek shelter in case the storm descends upon him. The last thing he wants is to have to hastily find cover like yesterday. While it sufficed, metal boxes were hardly an ideal place to seek respite.

After a few miles of walking, the track turns northeast, which would be taking him further from home, forcing him to abandon the tracks for some rolling hills, void of any trees. While most trees were burnt to a crisp during the calamity that claimed this world many years ago, the few that remained have long ago been used for firewood.

He plods along the desolate landscape, eyes sharp for movement of any kind. He finds that he is having to concentrate hard now to stay alert as his mind is fatigued. He lifts his feet slowly and steps gently, making no noise, part of his training. In fact, even when he is at home, he walks silently, even in combat boots. It is so engrained in him that he actually has to concentrate if he wants to make noise when he walks. It's just another facet of his robotic consistency that was beaten into him throughout years of regimented indoctrination.

Being downwind he smells it well before he sees it as visibility is limited. It's the scent of a struggling fire, likely the result of damp materials trying to burn. He now knows that others are close by so he goes into stealth mode, which isn't that much different than his normal way of moving other than he is now even more alert to any danger. He continues forward, climbing a steep grade, stopping at its apex for a good vantage point. A small campfire has been sparked to life. He can see the smoke now as one person is tending the fire, trying to keep it lit.

He carefully descends the steep rocky grade keeping veiled by the rocky topography to his right, his senses alert for any danger that might befall him. When he gets close enough to see the camp better, he spots three figures, all appear to be male, huddled around the fire. Each seems to be well geared against the weather with thick, heavy coats and dirty, wool hats. They also know enough to pick a campsite in front of what is left of an old van, which will offer some measure of protection if the skies open up.

Mason squats on his haunches, watching carefully for nearly 30 minutes, his acute hearing taking in everything. When his audibility implants were first activated, he thought he might go mad from the constant, low-pitched hum that unceasingly echoes in his head when there is complete silence. His hearing is increased four times that of a normal person and self-adjusts so that loud sounds are heard at a normal volume, but whispers can be heard easily. While it was something he hated when they were first activated, he has come to rely upon his enhanced hearing, something that has saved his life more than once.

None of the men move much, revealing little, conserving energy and trying to stay warm. While they most certainly have weapons of some sort, Mason doesn't see any guns. Their conversations reveal even less as no more than a few grunts are uttered. Maybe they have finally turned into animals, Mason finds himself wondering. He definitely doubts any of these individuals have what he seeks, but his job is to look, not to guess. The list of skills he is searching for has been committed to memory and now he needs to once again put himself in danger if he is to follow orders. He can feel his pulse quicken as he knows that these encounters have a tendency to go bad quickly as everybody out here can be deadly.

After watching for a while longer, Mason decides to proceed about his mission, putting on his backpack, but leaving his heavy bag hidden in a ditch. While most of his provisions are now gone, he does have enough food to last at least one more week, two if he rations them carefully. But he hopes it won't come to that.

He slowly, but not quietly, moves down the hill, now out in the open, purposely making enough noise to be heard. The three men jump to their feet when they hear him, turning and getting into defensive postures. Mason watches closely to see if any of them brandish a firearm. He is relieved to see they only have clubs and one has what appears to be half of a shovel.

"Hello," Mason shouts. "May I come and warm myself by your fire?"

None of the three men answer, so Mason continues forward, slowly. In a situation like this, it is paramount not to make any sudden movements, so Mason keeps his hands out and visible to show that he is not a threat. The three grizzled men, each with long, filthy beards and missing teeth, scowl at Mason as he moves closer, stopping just at the edge of the camp.

"If you men will allow me the opportunity to warm myself by your fire, I have a container of peaches, untainted and safe, that I will gladly share with you."

The men turn and whisper something to each other, their beady eyes and windburned faces showing distrust.

"If you will allow me, I have the peaches in my pocket. May I reach in my pocket to get them out?'

The largest of the three men takes two steps forward, holding what appears to be the metal leg of a table, and nods his head. Mason slowly moves his left hand down to the left side of his overcoat and eases his hand into the pocket. Then, he gently removes the clear, container of peaches and holds it up for them to see. All of their faces light up as this is likely the most food they've seen in a very long time.

"I am happy to share these with you. All I ask is that I can warm myself by your fire and have some companionship."

Then, after staring at Mason for several seconds, the largest man, the one that Mason has already ascertained as the leader by his stance and interaction with the others, waves him closer. Mason has noticed that there is always an alpha in every group. Mason forces a smile and walks close, rubbing his hands together to get some circulation going. It's all a charade, a carefully orchestrated act that Mason uses so he doesn't seem too formidable. He hunches as much as he can, trying to look smaller. He even tones down the timber of his voice to try and sound harmless. Sometimes it works, sometimes it doesn't.

"Thank you. I appreciate your hospitality."

The large one steps aside, allowing Mason passage to the fire. Mason walks cautiously, moving slow, even putting on a fake limp to convey weakness, acting like he's only looking at the fire, but actually keeping all three in his peripheral vision, which is also enhanced and allows him to see more than 180 degrees at all times.

As he gets closer, dancing in the flickering shadows from the fire, Mason sees a human leg bone on the ground. From the size of it, the person was small, likely a tiny woman or a child. His vast experience in such situations tells him all he needs to know as these grunting savages have evolved into the worst of what is remaining in the world. They are no longer human; desperation has transformed them into cannibals.

As Mason passes the first man, getting close to the fire, he has already prepared himself for the inevitable. And then it comes.

The short man to the right is jumpy and moves too quickly. In such a situation, a well-coordinated attack is necessary, but this man is too eager, lunging toward Mason's legs in an attempt to take him down. But Mason is ready. With lightning reflexes from inhumane training methods, Mason grabs the back of the man's head with both hands and thrusts his knee up as hard as he can while pulling the man's head down. The result is a bone-crunching, splintering sound as the man's nose, cheekbone and eye-socket shatter, dead before he even hits the ground.

Mason turns in a flash, just in time to evade the swing of the club from the larger man. The third man, holding the shovel, comes in from the right, but his moves are slow and clumsy, weak from malnutrition. Mason snaps out a front kick, knocking him down. The large man lets out an animalistic howl as he swings wildly with a one-handed motion, but the club clanks to the frozen ground, his hand and half of his forearm still clinging to the handle. The large man drops to his knees, mouth gaping open in pain as he cradles the stump where his arm used to be, tendons wiggling like headless snake bodies. He looks on in horror as his own crimson blood sprays the campsite. Mason used his machete, that he keeps concealed along the front of the long coat, allowing him to reach it instantly when needed, severing the arm in one, swift movement.

Even though these men deserved what happened to them, Mason has no interest in watching or prolonging their suffering. He wastes no time, taking a step and a second hard slash, lacerating the throat of the suffering man, who drops to his back, making a hoarse gurgling sound, dead in seconds.

The man with the shovel, still wheezing from the kick to the stomach, scrambles to his feet and scampers away, making the sound of a frightened lemur, scurrying off into the landscape. Mason's training tells him to pursue him and kill him. He even pulls his handgun and aims it at the back of the man's head, producing a red dot from the laser site, but he doesn't pull the trigger. A decision that is his and his alone. Instead, he watches the man try to run, falling three times before cresting a small hill. He's not worth a bullet. He won't survive anyhow. Nobody will.

After taking a moment to survey the situation, he cleans his machete off on the man whose face he caved in and who died instantly when bone fragments from his face impaled his brain. Mason then moves over to a ratty blanket that has been fashioned into a bag and opens it. He finds a couple of spoons, a can opener, two dented and worn steel cups, and two cans of food, neither with a label. He takes a handheld device out of his jacket pocket and waves it over each can, one getting a high reading for radioactivity, the other a much lower reading. But, since Mason is so close to home and still has some supplies left, he leaves it all.

After checking both men for anything useful, discovering that neither has anything he needs, he moves back to his original hiding place, hoists his pack onto his back and moves on.

CHAPTER FOUR

From the look of the debris, Mason is approaching what was once a small town. Not much is left, but there are a few, blackened buildings that partially are still standing. This is when he must remain diligent as there are many hiding spots. A rusty, steel sign is on the ground in front of a cement block structure that is half standing. He can just make out the writing and it reads *Service Station*. He examines the inside of the structure, but it has been picked clean of anything useful, so he continues along what was once a street with buildings lining both sides.

As he navigates around the rubble, he sees a partially standing, brick building with concrete lions on either side, which are chipped, cracked and worn. A sign on the building is barely legible, but Mason can partially make out the word "library." While the roof is gone, like most buildings, this structure is the one that is by far the most intact. After moving through the entire space and ascertaining that it is indeed abandoned, he starts sifting through the debris. While all the chairs and tables are gone, along with the shelves and books, long ago burned for warmth, he kicks through some rubble and he does find an obscure paperback novel, with a torn cover and water damage, but still mostly intact. He flips through it, imagining how many other people had fingered through this same copy over the years before the world went to hell. The book is called "Siddhartha," and he has never heard of it and knows nothing about it. While there is a vast library at home with just about every book a person could ever want, Mason puts this tattered copy in his pocket. He's not even sure why he does it. Maybe it's because this book is a survivor, like him. Too tough to be destroyed.

Further down the street, he finds a partially standing, brick structure that was clearly a store of some kind. While just about everything is gone, he does find some screws and nails, dented paint cans, steel wool, weather stripping, a pack of 9-volt batteries and a few other odds and ends. This is likely what was once known as a hardware store. He shoves the batteries and steel wool into his pocket and then sifts through the rest of the space, finding nothing of consequence.

The wind has picked up, as it often does before nightfall, forcing even Mason to shudder against the icy conditions. Mason explores what is remaining of the small town, carefully looking through the few remaining structures, none with roofs, a couple with partial brick walls still standing. One of the buildings used to be a bar and while there isn't a drop of liquor remaining, having long ago been scavenged, there are tin signs scattered about with words like "Coors," "Miller" and "Budweiser" on them. The thought of people traveling to a central location to sit together and drink beverages seems archaic to him. What purpose did it serve? Just another in a long line of things about the former world that he will never understand.

After finding nothing of use and confirming that the area is void of human life, he decides that with it being late in the day, this will be home for the night. The temperature has begun to plummet by the minute and full darkness will be upon him soon.

Of the limited amenities available, he chooses to go back to the service station because he noticed that it has something that was once known as an oil pit carved into the concrete floor. Once used so attendants could change the oil on cars, Mason drags a heavy, steel worktable, without any legs, over to the oil pit, laying it across the top. This will make a safe spot as the sky looks foreboding and the last thing he wants is to get injured or killed by icy projectiles when he is so close to home.

After setting up his tent in the pit, having a meal of dried, beef jerky, green beans and some water, he settles in and turns on a small flashlight. Usually, he only uses the flashlight when absolutely necessary, opting to save the batteries.

But on this night, he actually has some entertainment and decides that since he is nearly home, he can use the light to read this worn book that he found in the old library. While Mason reads occasionally, he wouldn't call himself an avid reader. But he feels compelled to explore a few pages to see what it's all about. To his surprise, he is quickly drawn into the story as he connects very much with the main character, Siddhartha. This man is also a lonely wanderer who walks the Earth. The only difference is that the book character is searching for the meaning of life, Mason mostly finds nothing but death. But still, he stays awake much longer than he usually does, comforted by an author who has been dead for more than 100 years. Somehow, he feels connected to the world through these words, reading the entire book in just a few hours, finding himself saddened when the story is over and the adventure has ended. In the end, Siddhartha finds the meaning of life, something Mason doubts he will ever have the opportunity to discover.

Mason flicks off the small light in the tent, falling asleep to the adventure of a lifetime told in less than 200 pages.

CHAPTER FIVE

Weary, not so much physically, but mentally, Mason trudges on, a northwestern wind stinging and drying out his eyes, prompting him to put on a black, tactical mask. It's been three days since he killed those cannibals and made camp in that oil pit, and he hasn't seen another person since then. With no precipitation, Mason has removed his overcoat, stowing it in his pack, allowing him better freedom of movement.

This, the final leg of his journey, can't end soon enough. He is beginning to see the landmarks near his home, such as the familiar mountain range with its deep valleys and knows that he is getting close. Last night, Mason set up camp in a small concrete tunnel that was once used to redirect water runoff from a small stream. He did have to drag out the skeletal remains of two, mostly decayed human corpses that previously sought shelter and perished in this terrible world.

It's good that he found that spot as his instincts were correct and a storm pounded the region during the night, the hollow shelter echoing from the relentless impact of large, frozen bombardments that regularly pummel the landscape. While he can barely remember the time before this became the norm, he has been told that hail was once relatively rare and usually quite small, something that occurred during warm months. But graupel, as it is called, is a term used to explain frozen accumulation that falls in the winter. These used to be quite small and harmless. But that is no longer the case. With a planet now in disarray after being violated by man, these murderous, icy attacks from the heavens batter the Earth often, sending frozen balls that can be as large as a human head to the ground. They are just another in a long list of ways to die in this world. The ground is littered with the shattered remnants of these icy cannonballs that regularly bash the landscape and explain why most structures that weren't destroyed during the final war, no longer have roofs.

It will be good to have some time to rest and enjoy the company of others before his next outing. This latest mission seems pointless, but they have their reasons and Mason will follow his orders. And if they instruct him to go out again, for a month, or a year, then that is what he will do. A soldier who has been trained to succeed at all costs and the pride of the Legion, Mason will always carry out his mission.

Sometimes he wonders what it would be like to say no. To look a commanding officer in the eye and tell him "no." It's something he has never really done. He imagines what it must feel like to be in charge of his own actions. Of course, out here, in this desolation, he does pretty much what he wants, but all of it ultimately stems from orders. Is he even capable of making his own decisions? He never has. It's somewhat troubling but philosophizing about a myriad of subjects is one way to keep from losing one's mind out here. Other than the occasional confrontation with random survivors, he spends countless days on end alone, just walking and exploring.

Earlier in the trip, Mason's senses were sharp, his mind alert, but the rigors of this outing have dulled all of that. Now, he wills his body forward, lost in daydreams. He thinks about the pleasing form of the physician's assistant at home and how she smells. The taste of fresh brewed coffee served in piping hot mugs at the café he frequents. And the smell of fresh bread each morning that Hans makes at the bakery. Warm, buttery bread is the first thing Mason plans to eat when he returns. Maybe a whole loaf, slathered with the homemade, garlic butter that Hans is famous for creating. Peach pie, his warm bed, a hot shower, the amenities of home are calling to him like a beacon.

As he ascends a small grade consumed by the pending comforts of home, he clumsily is out in the open when he sees at least half a dozen people, less than 50 meters away, tending a small fire as fuel to burn is becoming less and less available. He drops to his chest, scrambling to his left to seek cover from some rubble that was once a structure of some sort. How could he have been so careless? Had they seen him? It would be a miracle if they hadn't. While the mask offered respite from the relentless wind, he never smelled the fire.

He sits motionless for nearly a minute before finally poking his head out around the edge of a rock. With no accumulation at the moment, visibility is fairly clear and if they had been facing toward him, he would have easily been spotted. But it seems that luck was with him today. He must be more careful. Fatigue is a poor excuse for getting dead.

He removes the mask and from this vantage point, he will watch and listen for a while, as he always does, learning as much as he can about the group, searching for signs of intent, potential weaknesses and for one of the objects of his mission.

Unfortunately, the wind is coming in from his back, while he is hunkered down behind a pile of rubble, feeling the full brunt of the freezing conditions. Therefore, there is no protection from the cutting wind. In no time at all, without moving to keep warm, his core temperature will begin to plummet. He doesn't dare start a fire and can't risk trying to get the tent up. Normally in such a situation, he would backtrack a bit, searching for a better position to conduct surveillance and a safe spot to make camp. Plus, there is no cover anywhere and while the sky looks calm, Mason knows that the weather can change quickly.

While it is difficult to tell when evening is approaching as all day has the look and feel of twilight, Mason knows he has less than 90 minutes to make his move. He understands he should retreat, wait out the night, and come back in the morning. His training, not to mention his instincts, is telling him how to proceed. But he is tired, wanting only to return home as soon as possible. By delaying, he will cost himself yet another day in this hellhole. He recognizes that he is becoming reckless, but is desperate for some rest, and therefore he is ignoring what he knows is the best course of action. So, he makes the rash decision to approach the camp tonight, without having the proper time to access potential threats.

Mason retreats several hundred meters, finding a good spot, he hides his bag, only taking a jar of fruit for an offering. He puts the long coat back on and then marches back to their camp, this time noisily. When he gets close, he keeps hunched just a bit, hiding his 6-foot-2-inch muscular frame as much as possible, veiled by the large, dirty overcoat. He begins walking toward the camp, hands in the air to show he means no harm. As he gets closer, he sees five men and a child. It's the largest group he has found in quite a while. The fact that they have a child with them is a good sign. It likely means that they aren't cannibals. But the group makes poor sentinels as they never do spot him. He could easily kill them all before they even realize where the shots came from. But that's not why he's out here, so instead, in the most jovial and non-threatening tone he can, he shouts out "hello."

The group scurries around, seemingly aimless, it's almost comical to Mason. He thinks to himself that it's amazing they're still alive being this unorganized, not to mention the poor campsite location. If a rival group with bad intentions had happened upon them, it would have been a slaughter. If the skies decide to attack, they will also be in peril. It's almost hard to take them seriously.

They finally gather up some clubs and what look like a couple of knives. The one man has grabbed a rifle, the only firearm Mason can see, and is now brandishing it in an unskilled manner, squinting hard, looking off in the wrong direction, likely with poor vision since optometrists are hard to come by since the apocalypse began.

“I mean no harm,” Mason says in his least menacing tone, still keeping his hands up but alert to roll to his right for cover if necessary. “May I warm myself by your fire? I have food to share.”

Four men have now huddled behind some rubble that barely conceals them, the other man has stayed put, his arm around the child who is nestled in close.

“I have fruit. Enough for everybody to have some.”

“Open your coat,” the one with the gun barks. “Slowly or I’ll blow your head off!”

Mason does as he is asked, unbuttoning his coat and holding it open so they can see. They cannot see the machete in the liner of the coat or the handgun hidden near the small of his back. Obviously, these are not trained soldiers of any kind.

“Come forward slowly. Move quickly and you are dead,” the same man shouts.

Mason moves cautiously forward, entering the camp. “I am going to slowly reach into my pocket and remove a jar of peaches. Is that okay?"

"Go ahead,” the same man, the oldest and obviously the leader, says. “But don’t try nothing.”

Mason gently pulls the jar out and sets it down on the ground and then moves away, keeping his eyes trained on the men.

Slowly, the men advance to the large jar of food. One of the younger ones picks it up and hands it to the older man. He spins the lid off and dips his finger in and quickly tests it. His eyes light up. It has likely been a long time since he has tasted fresh fruit. He plunges his hand into the jar, stuffing peaches into his mouth by the handful, eating half of its contents himself.

Mason tries to contain a smile, thinking about how easily he could have simply poisoned them if he had wanted to.

Still licking his lips, smacking them together like a hungry dog while never taking his squinty eyes off Mason, he hands the jar to one of the three, younger men beside him and all hell breaks loose as they begin fighting, struggling and rolling around on the ground, each desperately trying to get as much of the food as possible. The leader seems oblivious to this, moving forward and looking at Mason, keeping the rusty rifle, which Mason recognizes as a .22 caliber. It's a low caliber gun and from the look of it, possibly doesn't work. Mason also notices that the man's left eye is cloudy, likely a cataract, which confirms his suspicions about his poor eyesight.

"Pretty stupid to come in here like you done," he says.

"I know."

"What's to keep us from eating your food, then blowin' your head off?"

With that, the child, a girl about seven years old, whimpers.

"You shut her the hell up or I will," the leader growls, prompting the man, likely the father, to hold her tight to his body, making soothing sounds and stroking her hair.

"Well, if you shoot me, then you won't ever find where I keep the rest of my food. There is plenty more where that came from."

"Ah. So, it's a bargain you seek," the leader says, unfurling his lips, exposing a brown-stained Jack-O-Lantern smile. "What do you want?"

"Just companionship."

"Huh?"

"Just to be around other human beings. I have been alone for so long. I have plenty of food, but I am tired of being alone. Safety in numbers is what I say. I will share my food and I only ask to be in your company."

"That's all," the man says, squinting skeptically.

"That is all. I require nothing else."

By now, the other men have finally finished eating the food, and one is still sitting on the ground, a bloody lip for his trouble, digging his fingers into the empty jar, licking the final drops of juice from the sides.

"Well, I don't know stranger. I can't just let anybody into our camp. Where is this food?"

"Not far, but I won't be able to find it now. It's too dark. In the morning I will take you to my stash. That is, if we have a deal."

"Why should I believe you?"

"Well. I guess you have no reason to believe me. But what do you have to lose. I gave you a sample of what I have. And that's just one jar. I have more than 40 more. I just want a group to be with, you know, for safety."

The man rubs his chin, looking Mason up and down, acting as if he is trying to make an important decision. In reality, they are desperate and if this stranger has more food that was as good as that, then there is no way they will turn him away.

"Tell you what. You can stay here tonight. But we will be watching you, carefully. Try anything stupid and I will put a bullet in your brain."

"You mean stupider than me walking into your camp unarmed?"

The leader squints at him for a moment, then breaks into a hearty laugh that quickly turns into a hacking cough. The other young men follow suit, also laughing. For the first time in months there is laughter in the group. Having a belly full of fresh fruit with the promise of more on the horizon makes them all feel optimistic.

CHAPTER SIX

After sitting around the meager fire for a few hours, Mason has learned that the leader is a man named Butch Kerns. He would guess Butch to be in his late-40s. The three younger men, all likely in their early 20s, Brett, and twins Blake and Bobby are his sons. Before all of this, Butch owned a beer distributor and was quite proud to tell Mason about how he built some empire with his own two hands. At the prodding of his boys, he even told a few stories about how he swindled this guy or that guy in some deal. Mason plays the role, laughing and asking just enough questions to feed the man's ego. All just part of his training. In truth, Mason knows nothing of business and has never even had a beer.

Butch seems to rule with an iron fist, none of the boys, much smaller than their father, dare try to wrestle the power away from him. They are all small and weak, looking to their father for direction. It is likely that their stunted growth has to do with lack of nutrition during adolescence as they would've been just children when the world went dark.

Mason has made a mental note of the weapons at their disposal. So far, he has seen the one gun, several long knives, a couple of clubs and what appears to be what is left of a garden hoe. It has been Mason's experience that less and less people have firearms these days and the ones who do, often do not have bullets. The time of chaos that existed before this has exhausted most ammunition.

Mason has now moved over and sits beside the other man, whose name is Clark and while he has lost track of the date and even the year, Clark is in his late 30s, although it is difficult to tell sometimes because this harsh lifestyle has a tendency to prematurely age people. He has long, brown hair, slightly graying at the temples, and green eyes that are sunken in slightly as is the case with most people in the world who are suffering from malnutrition. He never strays too far from Lydia, a dark-eyed child who he keeps close at all times.

As it turns out, he isn't her father. The group stumbled upon her one day.

Now, with the auburn glow of struggling embers flickering, the father and two of the sons are now fast asleep. The other, obviously designated to keep watch, keeps slipping in and out of consciousness on the other side of the fire. This allows Mason a chance to speak to Clark, who is now cradling the sleeping little girl.

"Butch wanted to leave her, as did one of the boys," Clark whispers.

"You wouldn't leave her?"

"If you had seen her. Sitting in a pile of rubble, the corpse of a woman, possibly her mother, lying a few feet away. I just couldn't leave her like that. But now, I question if I did the right thing."

"Why?"

"The other two have plans in mind for her. They whisper to each other often when looking at her. The look on their faces is like something you would see in an animal. Their jaundice, yellow eyes bulge as they gaze at her, their black teeth grinning.

"I have told them I will let them die if they touch her."

"Let them die? What do you mean?"

"A couple of months ago, I was hunkered down in what was once a medical clinic. It was a rural facility where I worked and since we were not near a major city, the area wasn't nearly as hot as the big cities. Anyhow, when they came in, the two younger boys were very sick. Radiation poisoning."

"Are you a doctor?"

"Yes. I mean. I was. A researcher mostly."

"Researcher?"

"Yes. Hematology among other things."

"Hematology? What exactly is that?" Mason asks, even though he has a pretty good idea of what it is.

"It's basically the study of blood."

Mason has seen more blood than most, but he never really considered it as anything more than something that pours out when you shoot or stab somebody.

"For instance, a simple blood test can tell you more about a person's health than just about any other test," Clark continues.

"So that is your specialty?"

"That was my specialty. I hadn't treated anybody in quite a while until they broke in."

"And you treated them?" Mason asks.

"At gunpoint, yes."

"Tell me about it."

"Well. As you know, scavengers have long since pretty much picked this world clean of anything useful. For years, I lived like everybody else, trying to survive."

"What happened to your family?"

"I don't know for sure. But my parents and brother lived in D.C. I hear that was hit first. I was only a few years out of residency, living in an apartment.

"At the beginning, I tried to provide medical care for the people as best I could, you know, in the building and neighborhood I lived in. For a short while, since our town wasn't directly hit, the buildings were still standing. But soon, those were destroyed by a combination of people bent on destruction, and icy cannonballs dropping out of the sky. After a while, with all these people living like animals, stealing, raping, burning buildings and killing, it became too dangerous to be out on the streets, so I stayed hidden most of the time.

"People who weren't killed right way, soon either got sick from the initial disease, fallout, or from starvation. When all my supplies ran out and I couldn't find any more, I made my way to the clinic. Even though most of it had been scavenged, there was a lower level that was secured with multiple, heavy security doors. It's where the lab was. Mostly just supplies, but I went there."

"And that's where they found you?"

"Yeah. I had been there for months, hiding in the basement. There were even a couple of food machines in there that hadn't been touched. I ate stale pretzels, chips, crackers, candy bars and even soda. With all of the re-enforced steel doors down there, I guess I got a little too comfortable. I hadn't seen anybody in so long. I was out in one of the corridors when they broke in and caught me off guard. Not that I could've done anything anyhow."

"What happened?"

"They asked if I was a doctor. I said 'yeah.' The old man shoved that gun in my face and said, 'fix them or you die.'"

"Fix them?"

"Yes," Clark says with almost a smile. "While most of the mainstream drugs were gone, in the basement storeroom we had some specialty supplies. We had a protein-based medication we were working on that was largely experimental and was designed to promote the growth of white blood cells. I prepared it for them and administered it with a syringe. To my surprise, they both actually recovered. They are still going to die young from exposure. By the looks of their eyes, I suspect liver failure is already in progress."

"So, what, they dragged you along?"

"They were going to kill me after I treated them. But I convinced them that this is an ongoing treatment," Clark whispered. "I told them that without me constantly monitoring their conditions and changing up a medication mixture each day, that they will die."

"A lie?"

"A lie. But I had to think of something."

"Ah. So, you are a prisoner?"

"Yeah."

"And you treat them every day."

"Not really. I have a bag full of supplies that I brought with me when we left the clinic," Clark motions to a large, blue bag sitting near him. "Most of it is just saline. But they don't know any better. I administer fake blood tests, using an eye dropper to pretend I'm examining the blood each day. Then using a syringe, I inject them with some saline."

"Why didn't you all just stay there?"

"We did for a while, but the food machines were soon empty and Butch and his boys are trying to go south."

"South? Why?"

"Apparently someone Butch knows told him that south things are better."

"But they're not," Mason says.

"I know. But Butch isn't exactly the smartest guy, now is he?"

Mason nods his head in agreement.

"I couldn't help but notice that they didn't share any of that food with you."

"No. They have some cans of dog food they found when we came across an old, mostly destroyed building, which used to be a veterinarian's office. Me and Lydia just get a few scraps here and there. The only reason either of us is still alive is because these hillbillies think if I quit giving them their shots, they will die."

Mason takes a careful look at the now slumbering guard who is supposed to be watching him. He smirks to himself as he thinks about how easily he could, and probably should, just kill them now. But instead, he reaches into his coat and removes a small cloth bag and hands it to Clark. After a moment of trepidation, he opens it and sees five, small plums. Clark's eyes light up, having not seen anything so glorious in a very long time.

"Where? How did you get this?

"Eat some now, while they are sleeping. And give some to the girl, too, but make sure they don't see it or they will surely take it from you."

"I don't know what to say?" Clark says with thanks gleaming from his eyes as he takes a bite of the fruit, its flavor exploding in his mouth. Almost instantly he feels like he can sense the nutrients coursing through his body.

"Tell me about her? How is she? Is she healthy?" Mason asks.

"Obviously she is malnourished," Clark says, taking another small bite of the plum, trying to make it last as long as possible. "But she doesn't seem to be suffering from anything else at the moment. But what a terrible world she was born into. I just couldn't leave her to die. No matter what they said."

"How do they treat her?"

"For now, they have mostly been leaving Lydia alone. But I can see in their eyes that they are just biding their time. If anything happens to me, the horror this little girl will see is hard to imagine," he says, holding her tight. "You should not have wandered into this camp. You know that once you show them where your food is, they will kill you."

"I know."

CHAPTER SEVEN

First light used to mean something very different. The black sky would slowly change, there would be hues of purple, red, orange and yellow as the sun crept above the horizon. It was a magnificent time of the day. In these dark times, the blackness of night gives way to a murky, gray light that offers just enough illumination to see the barren, ugly landscape of this bleak orb, nothing more. It offers nothing to the imagination, like the dimmest of lights creeping into a dungeon, allowing the occupants half a day to see the horror of their situation.

"Is it much farther?" Bobby whines, taking deep, raspy breaths.

"No. We are close. Just over this next ridge," Mason says.

"That's what you said 10 minutes ago," he says.

"I promise. Not much farther."

Mason, Butch and Bobby set out early to retrieve Mason's promise of food and goods. Brett and Blake stayed back at the camp to watch over Clark and Lydia, as ordered by their father. Butch, while out of shape and wheezing, walks with authority and purpose, his relic weapon held securely in front of him. Bobby, weak and perpetually tired, lags behind.

"You say that you've got fruit?" Butch barks.

"The freshest you've ever tasted." Mason replies, walking just in front, leading the way. "And not just fruit. But vegetables and even some hard-boiled eggs."

"Eggs? How could you possibly have eggs?" Butch wheezes, stopping for a moment, using his question as an excuse to catch his breath.

"You are just going to have to trust me. You won't be disappointed. I promise."

"And how did you come into all of this food you supposedly have?"

"Oh, that will have to be my little secret, Butch."

"Well, this better not be a wild goose chase or else I will cut you down where you stand."

"I understand. You are a man not to be trifled with and I certainly don't want to be killed. The food is there. I promise. And you will keep your end of the deal? Allowing me the safety of being part of your camp?"

"I'm a man of my word."

The trio of men continue to trudge on, the cutting wind making each step arduous. In truth, Mason could have gotten them to the food much faster, but he took a long, roundabout way to get to the destination to disorient and wear down his new "friends." In reality, they are still quite close to their camp.

"Here it is. Up ahead," Mason says with a smile.

The three climb a little grade and then Mason, keeping one eye on Butch, disappears behind a large boulder. After a moment, he emerges carrying the heavy, green canvas satchel. He walks over to Butch and puts it at his feet. Butch greedily drops to his knees and rips open the bag, revealing the most food he has seen at one time in years. Jars of peaches, plums, oranges, tomatoes and yes, even eggs. There are also numerous cans, without labels, written on in marker. Butch quickly grabs one of the jars and after some effort, opens it and begins shoving handfuls of grapes into his mouth with animal-like slurping and growling sounds. Bobby clamors up beside him, kneeling down and grabbing a jar too. However, he is too weak to get the lid off.

"So, do we have a deal?" Mason says.

"Is this all of it?" Butch says, stopping for a moment and eyeballing Mason, who is now standing on the other side of the satchel.

"Oh no. I have three more bags, just like this one, hidden back in those rocks."

"Really?"

"Yes sir. So? Do we have a deal?"

“Well stranger. I’m afraid we do not.”

“Why not?” Mason says, without surprise.

Butch lets out a satisfied laugh, looking to Bobby, who is still struggling with the jar.

“Why would I take you into my camp? Sharing our resources doesn’t make any sense,” he says. “I have all your food now. You don’t have nothing else to offer. In my other life, I was a businessman. Nothing different here. Just business.”

“So, you are just gonna send me on my way, with no food or water,” Mason asks, which is his way of letting this man live.

Butch laughs again, followed by a hoarse cough.

“Well, I can’t have you sneaking back to our camp now, can I? You understand, right?”

“I see.”

“Surprised you’ve lasted this long out here being this gullible fella. It’s nothing personal, just business. Just survival of the fittest.”

Butch starts to level the gun at Mason but he is kicked in the stomach so hard that he projectile vomits the grapes in one, purple heave as Mason quickly snatches the gun from his grip without a shot going off.

“You have broken our deal. Consider those grapes as your last supper.”

Bobby clumsily gets to his feet to mount an attack but Mason takes the butt of the gun and caves in the side of Bobby’s head just as the spindly, young man pulls a dagger from beneath his coat. Mason tosses the gun to the side.

Butch scrambles to his feet, pulling out a long blade of his own that Mason didn’t see but suspected he had. Butch holds it in front of him in the unskilled manner of a man with no combat training, still laboring from the kick to the gut.

"I have no desire to kill you, but I don't care if you die. I am going to take Clark and Lydia with me. You and your two remaining boys can move on. You will get no food from me, but you will get to live."

"I gonna send you to hell!" Butch screams, stumbling forward, taking an awkward swing that Mason easily evades.

"You have made your choice."

Butch again lunges, taking a vicious swipe with the blade. Mason blocks the attempt, controlling the wrist with both hands, puts his back into Butch and then flips him into the air, slashing his throat with Butch's own blade in one, clean motion, sending him crashing to the ground in a heap. Butch squirms there on the ground, gurgling, holding both hands to his neck, blood spurting out between his fingers, his eyes crazed with fear and panic. It takes less than 10 seconds before he stops struggling and except for the occasional death twitch, he dies quickly. He didn't have to die. He chose to. Mason stands for a moment, looking at the corpse when his enhanced hearing picks up the sounds of a struggle.

Brett and Blake have been waiting for the opportunity to have at that little girl since they first came upon her a few weeks ago. While Clark thinks the only reason Butch allowed her to come along was because he threatened to stop treating his sons, he had another reason. While they are not yet cannibals, if times got too tough, it would have been an option.

The two youngest Kerns boys were young when the skies went dark, both virgins stumbling through puberty. But now, both are young men, still virgins, and even in the midst of all this misery and strife, they are still being guided by their hormones.

They have not been apart from their father since they found her. With their dad around, a man of treachery, but not without his own rules of conduct, they did not dare touch her. But with him gone now, and the camp in their charge, the urge to take her is overwhelming. They know not what they will tell their father. They have not thought that far ahead, their minds clouded by carnal lust.

Clark has seen that look in their eyes for some time, knowing that they wish to commit unthinkable atrocities to the little girl. He has done his best to watch out for her, but he has always known that at some point he wouldn't be able to stop them. He just didn't think it would be today.

While leaning up against a rock, huddled close to the fire, he must've dozed off. That was all the Kerns boys needed. In an instant they were on him, pinning him to the ground. Blake straddling him, sitting on his chest pressing a razor-sharp hunting knife to Clark's neck, pushing hard enough to draw blood.

"You move. You die," Blake hisses through blackened teeth.

"No. Don't!" he shouts, but Blake punches him in the mouth with his free hand three times, splitting Clark's lip wide open, his mouth filling with the coppery taste of fresh blood.

While both boys are small and weak, Clark is also suffering from severe malnutrition and dehydration, so he is no match for both of them.

Seeing that his brother has Clark under control, Brett, who was holding Clark's legs, turns his attention to Lydia, who is awake and terrified. She is too frightened to run or scream. She only sits, staring up at Brett with horror in her big brown eyes. Like an animal, Brett pounces on her, aggressively throwing her on the ground. Clark tries to wriggle free, but Blake digs the knife further into his neck, causing more bleeding.

Brett throws off his wrap, the cold not bothering him right now. At this point, conscious thought is gone. He puts his hand on her neck and she promptly bites him on the wrist with all her might. He howls in pain, yanking his bloody hand away. Angry, he postures up, pulls his fist back and prepares to punch her when suddenly, he stops.

"Brett. Brett!" Blake shouts.

His brother is motionless, less than 10 feet away, and before Blake can make any sense of it all, a red dot appears on his forehead, followed by a subtle hiss and a hollow cracking sound. Blake flips off Clark, landing on his back, a small hole in the front of his head, the back of his skull and brains blown all over the ground.

Clark scrambles to his feet, rushing over to Lydia and pulling Brett off her. Upon rolling Brett over, he sees a bloody hole where his left eye used to be. He picks up Lydia, holding her sobbing and trembling body close to his own, while covering her with an old, worn blanket.

Mason appears from nowhere, walking back into the camp, holding a handgun with a laser site down at his side. He surveys the situation for a moment before finally speaking.

"You can stay here if you want or you can come with me," Mason says calmly.

AUDIO 2:

Listen to me very carefully. I am going to explain everything to you. If you are listening to this, then I am dead. It's time for you to know the truth.

When the virus hit, it seemed no worse than any other and except for the fact that it was highly contagious, the symptoms were generally mild and, in many cases, those affected were asymptomatic. Like a Trojan horse, it infiltrated our planet without causing a major panic. Sure, countries took measures to curb the spread, without much luck, but soon the world just got used to it and went on with business as usual. After all, the mortality rate was less than one percent. In less than a decade, the virus ran its course and the world went on.

Nearly everybody was infected, most without any adverse effects. And life simply continued.

Once the virus saturated the world population, that's when scientists discovered the true horror of this disease. And by then, it was too late.

Much like the way a person infected with chicken pox lives with it in their system for years and even decades before it causes shingles, this virus also had a secondary function. Within 7 to 10 years after infection, the virus reactivates, this time with a fatal outcome.

It started with a headache followed by confusion and within 48 hours, the affected person became violent and unreasonable. Paranoia soon would take hold and for the next several days, each person became capable of untold violence. The virus causes continual brain swelling and during this, people became unreasonable and extremely violent. The affected didn't eat or sleep, they simply became homicidally paranoid and wanted to attack and kill as much as possible. After being a savage for five to sometimes as much as seven days in some cases, ultimately the affected person loses consciousness, slips into a coma and dies.

Anybody who gets the virus dies. It's 100-percent fatal. As with anything, there are anomalies. A small percentage of people, less than 3 percent, were immune to getting it. That was a surprise. It was thought that only those who were immunized would survive.

CHAPTER EIGHT

Mason, Clark and Lydia trek across the desolate landscape, hiking for most of the day, stopping only briefly for Clark and Lydia to rest. The terrain is difficult to traverse, but where they are going there are no roads. Finally, as darkness begins to engulf them, they stop so Mason can make a camp for the night. This evening, a dirty, sleeting drizzle soaked them to the bone before Mason found what used to be an old railroad trestle that has long since been destroyed. However, where it attached to the hillside, several steel beams imbedded into the rock created a pocket at the base that is eight feet deep. While it's not ideal, it will provide some cover and Mason knows he cannot push them any further tonight. Clark and Lydia collapse when Mason announces this will be camp for the night, both suffering from extreme exhaustion. Mason instructs them to get out of the rain, which they both do, crawling into the small cave to get out of the rain.

Mason serves them both some food, telling them to eat slowly as they haven't eaten much in a long while and too much too quickly will most certainly make them sick. Numerous times he must remind them to stop, allowing for digestion before continuing.

After ensuring that they have gotten some proper nutrition, Mason scouts around, finding scraps of sticks, petrified roots, a couple burlap sacks he found along the way, and even prying free part of a cracked railroad tie. Over the years, Mason has become an expert at finding anything that will burn to create fires when needed.

With a full belly and a slumbering, shivering child leaning into him, Clark can barely move as his aching limbs feel numb. He watches in amazement as Mason arranges the soaking materials into a pile at the edge of the opening to provide cover from the rain. Using his knife, he scrapes the surface of a three-inch, silver square object, collecting a pile of shavings. He then sprinkles the substance onto the center of one of the sacks. Mason creates a fire by aggressively rubbing the steel wool across the top of one of the 9-volt batteries he found, causing a reaction that lights the steel wool. While he has a small torch he could have used, his training tells him that you always preserve as much of your resources as possible. Therefore, the battery and steel wool make a great substitute, which is why he grabbed them from the old hardware store he stumbled upon. Once the wool is lit, he drops it onto the sack, which ignites into a furious, bluish flame, burning and crackling so hot that Clark must shield his eyes. It reminds him of his own father telling him to look away when he would weld in the garage. Memories that now seem almost unreal considering the state of the planet now.

In a matter of minutes, Mason somehow manages to turn a soaking pile into a roaring fire. Clark is mesmerized by this man, so capable and seemingly with no weaknesses.

"How'd you do that?" Clark asks.

"What?"

"The fire. How'd you get it to burn so quickly. I've never seen anything like that."

"Magnesium. It burns extremely hot."

"How'd you find Magnesium?"

"Got it from a friend."

"Friend?"

"Well. More of an acquaintance," Mason says in a haunting tone, having found the magnesium stick a few weeks ago when he pulled it off the recently deceased body of a man who tried to make Mason his dinner. It didn't work out for him. Clark chooses not to inquire any further.

Mason says nothing, all business, tending to the task at hand. He is compartmentalizing, something he has done thousands of times during his training. He is handling duties as if he is following a checklist.

Mason has seen a lot and is an expert in human behavior on the outside. While Clark and Lydia might not realize it, they are rare, much tougher than most. After all, most simply give up out here, almost welcoming death rather than dealing with the pain and fear of living in this nightmare. The fact that both are still alive is a testament to that.

The roaring fire feels amazing, but their wet clothes are still chilling them to the bone and must be remedied. Clark then watches as Mason sets up the small tent in the mini cave he found, turning on the heating element. Tonight, it will be for Clark and Lydia to share. They need it. Mason will simply sleep close to the fire. When the work is done, then and only then, Mason strips out of his wet clothes to sit and warm himself by the fire, bare-chested, his impressive physique highlighted by the dancing shadows from the fire.

Finally, after a long period of silence, just listening to the crackling fire, Clark finds himself silently crying. No loud wailing, just tears gently falling down his grimy face. Mason notices but says nothing. It takes Clark several moments to compose himself.

“Sorry about that,” Clark says. “Not sure why that happened.”

“It’s normal. It’s a letdown now that the danger has passed.”

“I just. I just wanted to protect her. In fact, that’s all that’s kept me going. And then, well, when those boys attacked. I … I just couldn’t protect her.”

Mason says nothing but Clark needs to talk.

“You probably think I’m such a weakling.”

“Not at all. The fact that you and Lydia are still alive shows that you are stronger than most. I have great respect for you and her. You did what was necessary to survive. The ability to survive out here is rare.”

"Yeah. By being a prisoner."

"By being a survivor. You did what you needed to do to keep yourself and her alive. Never apologize for that. Not when most don't have that kind of courage."

Clark ponders that for a few minutes. That was certainly not the response he expected. He always thought of himself as a frightened prisoner. He never thought of himself as a survivor.

"You seem to have a very unique set of skills," Clark says, the small alcove shimmering with light.

Mason says nothing.

"So, what is it you do? Or did? You know, before all of this?"

Mason doesn't answer. In truth, he doesn't know. One day he was a carefree child, the next he was alone, and before he knew it, he was found and was being trained to kill without remorse.

"I never got the chance to thank you for what you did back there."

Again, there is silence from Mason.

"As a doctor, I have seen people die before. But not like that. While I am grateful, I am also bothered by it."

"Good."

"Good?"

"Yeah. It means you are still human. You still have a soul. When it stops bothering you, then you become a monster, like me."

"But you had to do it. Those men were going to rape Lydia and then probably kill us both. You shouldn't carry any guilt over that."

"I don't. I wish I did feel some guilt or remorse or anything. But to be honest, I don't. That is the most troubling part about it for me. That I have become so numb to death and suffering."

The two sit in silence for several moments, Clark not knowing what to say, Mason feeling there is nothing to say.

"Get her into that tent," Mason finally says. "It should be quite warm in there now. Get her and yourself out of those wet clothes and throw them outside. I will dry them by this fire. There's a blanket in there. Use it."

"What about you?"

"I'll be fine. Get in there and get some rest. Tomorrow's hike won't be any easier."

CHAPTER NINE

The next two days of travel are hard on Clark and Lydia. Lack of nutrition has left them weak, something that will takes weeks and even months to recover from provided they can get some regular, decent food. While Mason tries to choose the easiest paths he can find, in truth, all of the terrain is difficult.

If he was alone, Mason could've easily made the trek in just one day, but his two charges are just unable to move any faster.

Clark tried to carry Lydia for a while, but he was unable to keep up, forcing Mason to carry Lydia on his shoulders while also lugging his equipment and the remaining food. Clark can't help but marvel at this man who saved them, so strong, so able. After years of living out in this terrible world, Clark doesn't know what it feels like to not live in constant fear, like a defenseless mouse just hoping a predator doesn't choose to take his life. Clark also appreciates the fact that Mason doesn't complain about the slow travel or make them feel as though they are a burden.

Mason is surprised that Clark doesn't complain but is downright shocked that the girl hasn't whined either. The conditions are difficult and both are weak from years of malnutrition, yet each have shown great spirit. It explains why they are still alive.

Periodically, they hike past the skeletal remains of those who lost their lives in this awful world. Other than the constant, howling wind, there is no sound. No people, no scent of fire, nothing but death all around. At this point in the journey, that is a very good thing. Mason doesn't want to have to deal with any more conflict. These two have seen enough and the last thing they need is to watch Mason kill anybody else.

For the past several hours, Mason has picked up the pace and even though he is carrying Lydia and all the gear, Clark can scarcely keep up. With less than an hour of light left, they enter an open field, their footfalls crunching the dead, petrified field of grass. Mason strides directly toward a rock formation in the middle of the field. Mason stops briefly, removing his hat and the rags around his face. He stands there quietly for a minute or two before then moving on. He leads them over to the rocks, which are about 20 feet high and 60 feet wide, guiding them over some lower spots, getting to the middle where there is an indentation. Mason finally stops, dropping his gear and placing Lydia on the ground. Clark, gasping for air, his heart pounding so hard that he can hear it in his ears, scrambles up next to him, dropping to his knees, trying to catch his breath.

Mason pops his head up and is scanning the horizon, his trained eye searching for anything out of the ordinary. He is looking for any motion, any sound, but he doesn't see or hear any. Still, he continues to survey the area.

"Are we going to camp here tonight?" Clark asks.

Mason doesn't answer, he just continues to scan the area, on the lookout, as always.

"What are you looking for? Is somebody following us?"

"No."

Clark wonders why they have not built a fire or tried to set up a campsite but has decided not to pester the man that has already saved them once. After waiting for close to two hours, the infrared cameras hidden in the rocks and scanning in every direction as the three are sitting in complete darkness, ascertains that they are indeed alone. Slowly, there is a low, grinding sound that echoes from inside the rock.

"What is that?" Clark whispers with panic in his voice. "We must go! We gotta hide."

"It's ok," Mason says evenly.

“The sliding sounds continues, followed by a hollow groan as an opening appears from the side of the rock in the indentation, right where Mason is standing. The opening grows until it is about three feet wide and four feet high.

“Be sure to wipe your feet before you come in,” Mason says in a voice that almost sounds jovial, with a mischievous twinkle in his blue eyes.

"You want us to go in there?"

"Sure. Why not?"

"No offense, but we don't know you at all. For all we know, you could be a cannibal or something."

Mason smiles, the first smile Clark has seen from him. It's quite handsome. He actually has white teeth, something Clark hasn’t seen in years.

"And you think I have been sharing all my food with you for what reason? Fattening you up?"

Mason wastes no time, crouching down and disappearing into the black sliver of the opening. Clark hesitates, turning and looking at Lydia, who has moved close to him and is looking into the dank doorway.

"Well. What do think?" he asks her.

She shrugs her shoulders, perhaps figuring that whatever is inside that rock cannot be any worse than what is outside, then quickly darts inside.

"Lydia!" he whispers. "Wait!"

But it’s too late, she is gone.

"Oh hell," he says, taking a deep sigh, having no idea what to expect. Finally, he gives in and enters the black space.

Seconds after all three get inside, the opening grinds shut again, plunging the space into total darkness. Clark feels his heart rate quicken, fear nearly overtaking him. He wants to shout out for Lydia but does not want to give up his position. After several more seconds, a pale, purplish light glimmers to life from a tiny fixture above, revealing the inside of the rock formation. Unlike the naturally occurring, rough rocks on the outside, the inside is quite another story, which is a square, small space with smooth concrete walls, ceiling and floor.

"What is this place?" Clark mutters to himself, gawking around the space, seeing the heavy, steel locking mechanism on the door.

"Watch your step," Mason says, motioning for Lydia and Clark to back up a few steps.

From the floor, where a circular perforation is barely visible, a manhole-sized slab of concrete begins to rise, making a smooth, masonic sound as it slides out of the floor. It takes nearly a minute to get the plug free, pushed up by four, circular, metal beams. More than four feet deep, the cylinder-shaped piece of concrete is hoisted clear of the floor, rising above a dark, ominous, circular opening in the center of the floor.

For a moment, everybody stands motionless until a yellowish, pale light suddenly blossoms from the hole. Mason kneels down beside the hole, seeming oblivious to the fact that there is more than a ton of concrete above his head. A metal ladder rises from the depths with a mechanical hum, not stopping until the top of its silver rungs are clear of the hole. Mason looks at Lydia and Clark with a smile and then quickly descends the ladder, disappearing into the hole.

Clark, with a knot in stomach and beginning to feel incredibly claustrophobic, helps Lydia onto the ladder and then, after taking one last look around the space, he too descends into the opening.

CHAPTER TEN

Only eight years old, the boy looks more like he's five with his emaciated, skeletal limbs and sunken-in face. His caramel-colored skin is covered in dirt and sores as he sits silently by the body of his father, whose body is still warm.

The two had been hiding in what had once been a fruit cellar before the skies went dark. While there was no food there, it was a welcome respite from the whipping wind and battered landscape. However, while escaping from two cannibals who had plans on making his son their dinner, Hector was cut badly with the metal blade of a rusty hoe. While he was able to wrestle the implement away and bash their heads in, the injury became infected over several days. By the time they found this little hideout, Hector already knew that he was in trouble.

For more than a week, Hector and Luis stayed hidden, using old sacks as blankets, as Luis tended to his father, dabbing his forehead with a wet rag to try to battle the fever.

Hector clung to consciousness by telling his son stories of life in a country called Guatemala, which is where Hector lived until his early 20s when he moved to the United States. He tells Luis about how he worked on a coffee bean farm, hand-picking the beans to be used to make what Hector calls, "the greatest coffee in the world."

Working alongside his two brothers and his father, he began on the farm when he was Luis's age. They would work all day in the hot, Guatemalan sun, for very little pay. But Hector explains that he was happy and how those were some great times with his family. Hector tells him all about the beautiful skies, mountainous landscape and unequalled sunsets.

Luis would ask his dad the same question every night.

"Do you think in Guatemala it is still like that?"

Even though Hector knows that it is not, he never tells him that this is a global calamity. He wants his boy to have something to hope for. Something to get him through each day in this hell on Earth.

Hector loved Guatemala, but when the country fell into a civil war of sorts, suddenly work was hard to come by and poverty became very prevalent. So finally, he and his brother immigrated to the states to find work, with the plan of saving up some money and bringing Hector's mom, dad and younger brother to join them. But the plan didn't work out as the planet began to tear itself apart.

One day, Hector's brother, Raul, attacked him with a baseball bat, trying to bash his brains in. The white part of his eyes had become orange and he was impossible to communicate with. Ultimately, with no other choice, Hector ended up stabbing his little brother in the head to finally stop him. Hector was never the same again.

Luis was born well after the world went to hell, something that Hector feels guilty about every day. When a companion that Hector was living with got pregnant with his child, both of them contemplated aborting the pregnancy. But both being of strict Catholic upbringings and who believed they were now living in the time of the tribulation, were unable to go through with it. So instead, Luis was born into this cruel world. Karen died just months after giving birth from organ failure due to fallout and for the past eight years, the two have been on their own.

Now, with his body slowly going cold, Luis kneels next to him, his tear-streaked face lining his grimy skin. What will become of him now?

Just hours after his father died, the heavy, metal door swings open and standing there is a large man in tactical gear with a gun on his hip and brandishing a rifle.

Luis cowers in terror as the man pulls out a flashlight and shines it into the fruit cellar, getting a good look at the young boy with his big, frightened, haunted, brown eyes.

“I suppose you will do,” the man says.

CHAPTER ELEVEN

It's at least a 30-foot descent to the bottom, the tube illuminated with that yellow light. The slow, Masonic slide of the floor plug can be heard being lowered back into place making it hard for Clark to get a deep breath as the thought of being buried alive is terrifying to him. Having never been good with closed spaces, he feels like he is being placed into a tomb and must concentrate on his breathing to keep from having a full-on panic attack.

The three are received in a long, concrete corridor by two people in all white bio-hazard suits. Their faces are hidden by masks and their breathing is raspy and artificial as both are wearing air tanks.

"Hi Rachel. Have you put on weight?" Mason says, morphing into more of a human by the second, a far cry from the all-business warrior he was on the outside.

"Bite me, Mason," an amplified female voice answers as she and the other person begin carefully running a metallic wand all over Mason, Clark and Lydia.

"They are checking us for any contamination," Mason says. "Neither of you better be trying to smuggle dope in here."

"The only dope in here is you Mason," Rachel says, getting a chuckle from Mason.

After a few more moments, the scan is completed.

"They are clear," Rachel says.

The other person in bio-hazard gear goes over, presses a button and yet another hatch hydraulically slides open with an echoing thud.

"Please follow me," Rachel says.

She leads them down the concrete corridor to a large, metal door. Rachel punches a long series of numbers into a keypad that triggers a clicking sound as the door is unlocked. Rachel opens the door and motions for them to enter.

With Mason leading the way, the trio of travelers enter a large, round room with four more metal doors.

"How long has it been since you've had a hot shower?" Mason asks Clark.

"Are you kidding?"

"Been that long, huh?"

"You two go in there and shower, the girl can go in this one," Rachel says.

Lydia clings to Clark's leg at the thought of being separated. Rachel immediately sees this and silently chastises herself for being so thoughtless.

"Of course, you may go with her if you wish," she says.

"Thank you," Clark says with relief in his voice.

"There is a red container in the corner. Remove all of your clothes and put them in there, securing the lid before you shower. Do you understand?"

"I do," Clark says.

"You will find a shampoo and soap combination in one large container. Use it liberally and rinse well. It is a special anti-microbial compound that will ensure that it kills any unwanted bacteria or fungus. But rinsing is vital or you will get itchy afterwards. Also, when you are done, there is a bottle of cream. Spread it on every part of your skin, and again, use it liberally because the soap is kind of harsh and can give you a rash."

"Okay." Clark says.

"There are clothes in the blue lockers in there of various sizes as well as sandals. You may put those on when you are done and then exit using the door marked exit. Do not come back out this door or we will have to do this all over again. Understand?"

"Yes," Clark says, having an overwhelming feeling that he hasn't felt in years. At first it takes him a minute to realize what that weird sensation is. It's déjà vu. Rachel recognizes his moment of confusion.

"Are you okay?" she asks.

“Uh. Yes. Sure. Just tired and this is all just a lot to take in.”

“Of course. That is totally understandable. I think you’ll both feel much better after a shower and some food.”

Rachel opens the door and the two enter before she closes it behind them. She walks over to another door and opens it.

"You too, Mason," Rachel says.

"What? By myself?"

"You’re a big boy. You can handle it."

"Will you come in and do my back?”

"Go,” she says, stifling a giggle. “I can damn near smell you through this mask."

Mason smiles again, the relief of being back home washing over him, making him downright jubilant.

“Yes ma’am,” he says, entering the room.

“Glad you’re back,” Rachel says as the door clicks shut.

Lydia and Clark do as instructed, getting rid of their clothes. They each go into a little alcove and the warm water cascading down their bodies feels downright euphoric. Clark feels like he could stay there forever. It's hard to believe he used to take it for granted. He never wants to get out. During the shower, which is the first time he has had his clothes off in a very, long time, he realizes just how skinny he has become.

Finally, having cleaned himself and having helped Lydia, who has become like a daughter to him, he applies the thick cream, rubbing it in the best he can before getting dressed in the soft, white cotton pants and shirts.

Opening the exit door triggers an ultraviolet, purple light bathing the short hallway in an eerie hue. After a moment of trepidation, Clark leads Lydia down the hallway. The door shuts behind them and he instinctively rushes back and grabs it, trying to open it again, but it is locked behind him. Trying to calm himself, slowing his breathing to keep from hyperventilating, he takes Lydia by the hand and walks to the next door.

“How many damn doors are in this place,” he wonders out loud.

Clark can feel the hackles beginning to rise on his back. “Don't panic” he tells himself, knowing that he has to keep himself together for Lydia’s sake. “Remain calm.”

After standing in the purple illumination for sixty seconds, which feels like an eternity to Clark who is freaking out, the lights shut off and the door at the other end clicks. Clark quickly grasps the handle and opens it, feeling a wave of relief. As quickly as he can, he hustles himself and Lydia through where they are received in a large, white room, with bright lights.

Sitting there, now wearing a blue jumpsuit, Rachel smiles warmly, her thick, curly, light brown, shoulder-length hair framing a healthy, tanned face with blue eyes and white teeth. With the exception of Mason, Clark hasn't seen anybody with white teeth in years, not to mention a tan.

"Welcome," she says, rising and coming toward them. "My name is Rachel. I am happy to meet you," she continues, reaching out and shaking his hand, then squatting down to talk to Lydia. "What is your name?"

"She doesn't speak," Clark says. "Her name is Lydia. At least, that was the name she had written on the front of a little notepad she had when I found her.”

"Oh. How sad. Well, don't you worry. There is nothing to be afraid of here Lydia. You are safe."

Rachel stands up and looks Clark in the eyes with a friendly smile.

"And your name is?"

"Clark. Clark Higgenbothum."

"Nice to meet you, Clark. I'm sure you want to go rest. But would you like to eat something first?"

"What is this place?"

"This was built before it happened."

"Who built it?" Clark asks, all of this feeling surreal to him.

"I really can't answer that."

"Are there others here?"

"Yes."

"How many? How many others? Survivors, are there ..."

"Please. Please. Somebody will try to answer all of your questions later. But this little girl looks like she needs a hot meal and a warm bed."

Clark looks at Lydia, standing next to him, her wet, curly black hair shining, her big, brown eyes heavy with fatigue.

"Yes. Of course, you're right. Where is Mason? I want to thank him."

"You will see him later. It is very late now. Why don't we get you guys a bite to eat and then I will show you to your room."

CHAPTER TWELVE

After nearly inhaling the best food he has seen in a very long time, consisting of fish, fresh greens and tomatoes, corn and even Jell-o, washed down with a cold glass of rice milk, Lydia and Clark are led to a short hallway with yet even more doors. Rachel opens one of them, revealing a small room with two beds, a dresser and several clean blankets.

"Please. Rest now," Rachel says. "If you need them, the restrooms are at the end of the hall, marked lavatory."

"Thank you so much for this."

"We are happy you are here."

"What happens tomorrow?" Clark asks, still in protector mode, holding Lydia close to him.

"Tomorrow?" Rachel asks.

"Yes. I mean. What next?"

"I want you two to sleep in as long as you want. When you awaken, return to the common area where you just ate, and you can enjoy breakfast."

"Then what?"

"We will talk tomorrow. You both need to get some rest. Sweet dreams," she says in a soft tone, turning a dial on the wall, dimming the lone light fixture on the ceiling before shutting the door.

Standing, consumed in thought, Lydia finally stirs Clark from his daze by tugging on his shirt sleeve.

"Oh. I'm sorry honey," he says. "He leads her over to one of the beds, scooping her up and laying her down. He then fluffs her pillow a little and then tucks her in with one of the blankets, although it is not necessary as the room is nice and warm, the linens smelling fresh and clean.

"Are you comfortable?" he asks.

She nods her head yes and, for the first time he has seen, she actually smiles. His heart nearly melts. While this is not his daughter and he never had any real desire in his life to be a father, by the crazy circumstances that this world has thrust upon them, that is his role. Having never been a very compassionate person before, being in her charge, responsible for keeping her safe, has awakened a nurturing side that he never knew existed.

He gently strokes her forehead, coaxing a long yawn and a satisfying sigh from her. He watches as her flickering eyelids flutter for a few moments before shutting for good. He then gently stands up, moves over to the other bed and eases onto the soft mattress. After sleeping for so long on the hard frozen ground, this feels like a warm cloud, caressing him. The soft pillow, gently supporting his head is the last thing he remembers. Even with all of the questions bouncing around his head, he is unable to stave off sleep. He never even manages to pull a blanket on himself, asleep in a matter of seconds.

-

Clark sits up instantly with a gasp, a scream caught in his throat, his mind reeling, trying to make sense of what is going on. Where is he? Oh yes, he remembers. He turns and looks for Lydia, her bed is empty, the covers barely even ruffled.

"Lydia," his dry throat croaks out. "Lydia!" he shouts louder this time, his vocal cords breaking loose with his second attempt.

He leaps to his feet, goes to her bed, pulling at the covers, hoping she is just hidden under the thick blankets. Clark then drops to his knees and checks under her bed. He then crawls across the floor and looks under his own bed. She is gone. Is it daytime? Nighttime? How long has he been sleeping? Is he a prisoner?"

Panic now engulfing him as he rushes to the door, he grabs the handle and begins pulling. Locked. He can't get out.

"Lydia!" he screams.

He continues to pull at the door, finally realizing that the door actually swings out, something he didn't quite think of in his cloudy, frightened state of mind. He slams the door open and begins running down the well-lit hallway, around a corridor, seeing nobody. He darts into the common area where he sees Rachel pouring a cup of coffee.

"Where is she?" he shrieks.

"What?" she says, spilling some of her coffee as he obviously startled her.

"I said where is she? Where is Lydia?" he demands.

Rachel gives an understanding perch of the lips and points to the corner of the room where Lydia is sitting, enjoying a plate of scrambled eggs and some orange juice, her eyes bright, her face looking rested.

"Lydia, I couldn't find you. I... I was so worried. I…" he says, rushing over to her and hugging her awkwardly as she tries not to spill her orange juice.

"It's okay Clark. You have been through a lot. Your reaction is totally understandable," Rachel says with a reassuring tone.

"I just. I ..." Clark stammers as he stands back up, finally releasing Lydia who goes back to eating her breakfast.

"She woke up and mustn't have wanted to wake you. About an hour ago I was sitting here, going through some medical charts, and she just wandered in. I asked her if she was hungry and she nodded. So I gave her some food. That is actually her second plate. A good appetite is a great sign."

"Lydia honey, don't ever do that again. Wake me next time, okay? I was worried."

"Clark. She is totally safe here. You don't have to worry anymore. It's not like it was on the outside."

"How long have I been sleeping?"

"Close to 13 hours."

"What? No. It couldn't have been more than two or three."

"That is not unusual. She slept more than 12. When you have been living like you were, you likely never got any good sleep. Your body needed an extended rest."

"I've never slept that long in my entire life."

"You can expect that for a while. Your body needs it."

"I'm sorry. For my reaction just now. I … just."

"No need to apologize," she says calmly, trying to give him some comfort, knowing his psyche is letting down now. "How do you feel?"

"I... I don't know. I don't know how to feel."

"From what Mason told us, things were rough for you and her out there. You being her protector is a source of great anxiety. It is only natural that you are still feeling that. It will take some time before you can relax, but trust me, it will happen."

"It's just so much to take in. I … I don't know what to say."

"Would you like something to eat?"

Clark, out of breath and feeling foolish, wants to curl up on the floor and cry like a child. A letdown, a mix between fear and relief. But he takes a moment to compose himself, not allowing himself to crumble.

"Got another one of those?" he says, pointing to her coffee cup with a shaky hand.

"I sure do," she says, going over to the counter and pouring him a fresh cup. "Cream? Sugar?"

"You have cream and sugar?"

"We do."

"Then … both, please."

CHAPTER THIRTEEN

Standing at attention in front of a metal table in a room with dull gray walls and a matching shade of paint on the concrete floor, Mason, shoulders back, head held high, wearing beige fatigue pants and a matching shirt with his name printed above one of the pockets, stands stoic. His square jaw is set and his blue eyes remain fixed on the large mirror behind Schmidt. He has slipped back into soldier-mode and will remain still and quiet until spoken to.

Normally, Commander Victor Schmidt will allow one of his men to stand silently for a long time, squirming under his intimidating stare, sweating the consequences of some undesired act. But Schmidt knows that is a waste of time with Mason, a nearly perfect soldier with only one flaw: Compassion. For all his training, all his physical and mental attributes, his surgical upgrades, they have never been able to fully remove compassion from his psyche. Sure, he will kill without remorse when provoked, but he will not murder in cold blood and he has a bad habit of bringing in strays.

"Why do we keep having this conversation?" says Schmidt, who doesn't particularly care for Mason, preferring to have mindless automatons who follow every order without fail.

"The soldier does not understand the question, sir," Mason barks in a loud, rough voice that infuriates his commander.

"You know what I mean," Schmidt says, slapping his thick palm on the steel table.

Schmidt is in his late 40s, short and paunchy, with tightly cropped blonde hair with flexes of gray throughout, and heavy, wrinkled eyelids that always looks partially closed over bulging, light, green eyes. Sitting at the table, his beige shirt rolled up to his elbows reveal a pair of chubby forearms. He stares angrily as he searches Mason for answers.

"I successfully completed my mission, sir."

"Your mission was to bring back a physician. Not some spindly girl, another mouth to feed."

"Sir, it was the soldier's opinion that the doctor would not come alone. He would not leave the girl to fend for herself."

"Then you should have eliminated that variable."

"Sir?"

"Seemingly every time we send you out, you bring back your target, plus-1."

"The soldier apologizes for his error."

"Yes. You do. You always apologize and then you always do it again. How many has it been? If it wasn't for the fact that you are so highly valued, the punishment you would receive would be severe."

"Sir. The soldier is prepared to gladly accept any punishment that his Commander feels is necessary."

"Yes, yes. I know. You will take whatever comes your way, your mental and physical strength easily overcoming any punishment we could come up with. But do you understand that, while we have supplies, they are not endless? These decisions are not for you to make."

"Sir, yes, sir."

Schmidt fancies himself as a lifelong soldier, but in reality, he has never seen combat in his life. He went to an exclusive military university where they played soldier and then was part of a reserves program on the outside where his lineage set him up as a base commander. Just days before the world fell into chaos, reporting as ordered, he went to the coordinates his father provided. This has been his existence ever since.

"Okay," Schmidt barks. "What about it. What have you seen?"

"Sir, in the 49 days on the outside the soldier covered more than 300 miles, engaging just 14 groups, 63 total people. 41 men, 18 women and only four children."

"And how were they living?"

"Most are traveling by day, in search of food."

"Food?" Schmidt asks.

"Yes. Of the 14 groups, all were desperate. Nine appeared to be cannibalistic, three more were hostile and only two were friendlies, sir."

"How did these encounters conclude?"

"The friendlies offered what little they had to me. But none had the necessary skill set defined. A group of 4 and another of 3."

"The others?"

"The 12 others who I engaged were not friendlies. They all attacked, some immediately, some later."

"How many casualties?"

"26."

"Why let the others go?"

"They didn't attack with their groups, but instead retreated."

Schmidt frowns at Mason for a few moments. While Mason is the most capable of any of the Legion members, he has a weakness that Schmidt hates. He tends to break with protocol. It's a small thing, but for a man like Schmidt, it comes off as insubordination.

“You know, they could have gone for weapons and came back to attack you later, right?”

“It was the soldier's opinion that none of them had the skill set or desire to engage in more confrontation and posed no real risk.”

“If you had killed them, you'd probably be doing them a favor,” Schmidt says with a roll of the eyes.

“Sir?”

“Never mind,” Schmidt says before pushing himself away from the table and standing. The short man snaps out a firm salute.

“Submit to a full physical, then decontaminate again and you may go home."

"Sir, yes, sir." Mason barks, returning the salute before turning crisply and exiting the room.

Schmidt turns and looks at the mirror with a shake of his head at the others in the observation room.

CHAPTER FOURTEEN

"So, I understand that you're a doctor?" Rachel asks as she feels around Clark's neck with a pair of rubber-gloved hands.

"I am?" he says, sitting on a small table, wearing just his white pants in a small examining room with cinderblock walls painted white. He feels embarrassed as he looks down at his scrawny body. While he was never what you would call buff, he exercised regularly and had a healthy build.

"Mason mentioned it. I feel kind of silly giving a physical to a doctor."

"Why? It's pretty tough to give yourself one. Besides, out there, I never bothered to check myself out. For a while, I think I was kind of hoping for death."

Rachel says nothing, uncomfortable with his statement.

"I'm sorry. I didn't mean to make it sound like that," realizing just how rusty his social skills have become.

"No. Don't apologize. I mean, I can't even imagine what you have been through?" she says.

"Well. I'm sure you saw some of the same stuff."

"No. I really haven't. Right before it all happened, I was instructed to come here. I have been inside since before it began."

"You have?"

"My father was a high-ranking official."

"In the military."

"Not exactly," she says with a purse of the lips that tells him there is probably a lot of layers to all that created such a facility.

"That's pretty cryptic," Clark says, eliciting a chuckle that prods Rachel to explain a bit further.

"To be honest, I still don't know all of the details. I know that he was part of an organization that believed a contingency plan needed to be put in place in case of a disaster."

"Disaster?"

"The rumor is that an astronomer had spotted a doomsday asteroid that might impact the planet. The story I heard is that he even had a date, something like 24 years from the time he discovered it."

"I remember that asteroid. It was the size of Colorado. You could see it in the sky for weeks and it was pretty spectacular. But it was nowhere near hitting our planet," Clark says.

"They say that as it turned out his math was off by about 20 million miles," she says. "In space terms, I suppose that could be considered a near miss."

"So, this place was built as a bunker in case of impact?" Clark asks skeptically.

"I guess. At least that's what they told me when I asked the same questions that you are asking now."

"And your father?" Clarks asks.

"My dad was always traveling. All I know is that he worked in finance. My mom said he was extremely successful. A very important man, she told me. He was instrumental in constructing this place. I never even knew about it until a few days before things got bad. I got a call from him and he told me to pack two bags and that a car was coming to pick me up. I was instructed not to ask any questions but to get in the car when it arrived and go."

"You said your father 'was' part of an organization."

"Yes. He was working out of the country at the time. He couldn't make it back in time."

"I'm sorry."

"And your mom?"

“Dad told me that she would meet me there.”

“But she didn’t?”

“No. Neither of them made it. I hear that things on the outside got very bad very quickly.”

“Not getting a chance to say goodbye is hard. I often think about my parents and siblings.”

“I think that’s the hardest part. Not knowing.”

“I’m so very sorry.”

"Me too," she says.

"So, you never saw what it was like out there?”

"No. The closest I have ever gotten is when a few people like yourself are rescued and brought in. The stories from you and people like you paint a horrid picture. Really it is impossible for me to even fathom what the world has turned into in such a short time. I still dream about sunsets, rainbows and summer thunderstorms."

"You said others have been rescued."

"Just a few. Every once in a while, Mason and a couple of people like him go outside, always alone, and try to find people to bring back. Most return alone, and some, not at all."

"So that is what Mason does?"

"Yes. In part. He is sent out periodically. Not only to find people, but to access the situation. He then brings back a detailed report about his findings," she says as she removes a needle and inserts it into his arm. "I need to draw some blood so we can do some tests."

"You have a testing facility here?"

"Yes. We have a well-equipped lab."

Rachel carefully and efficiently draws three vials of blood before removing the needle and applying a cotton ball to the injection site.

"He seems very good at his job."

"Who?"

"Oh. Uh. Mason."

"You have no idea," she says with a nod of agreement.

CHAPTER FIFTEEN

Luis keeps trying to stay on his feet, but his naked body keeps getting knocked to the ground by the harsh spray of water coming from a high-pressure firehose. Every time he falls, the man shouts for him to get to his feet or turn around. Each time he does, the man sprays him again, knocking him back down. He can hear the man laugh each time he falls. Luis is shivering so hard that he can hardly breathe as the water is ice cold. The water pressure is so hard that he feels as though he is being stabbed with hundreds of needles.

The man who found him with his dead father has treated him like an animal. He entered the root cellar and grabbed him by the neck and dragged him out into the cold. He was forced to walk for days, with a burlap bag over his head, slapped by the big, angry man anytime he fell behind or stumbled. For days they traveled, stopping rarely, getting very little sleep. He was pushed and shoved, so tired that he was in a daze. During the entire ordeal, the man said no more than a few words, and those were simply blunt orders that if he didn't follow immediately resulted in being struck. Luis found himself wishing for death, silently praying to himself continually, begging for the Lord to take him so he could be with his father. Anything to end this suffering. Just when he thought he could go no further, they finally ended up inside some sort of structure. The sack was removed from his head and all of his clothes were ripped off and he was shoved into a corner with a floor that has a drain and the hosing began.

Finally, when the hose stops, the man comes in and douses him with a bucket of white, pungent powder that makes him choke. The man doesn't stop dumping the powder on him until he is completely covered. Luis is on his knees, choking from the harsh cloud.

He is then grabbed by the neck and dragged down a series of hallways until they come to a dark, corridor full of what appear to be jailcells on one side. Luis wipes his eyes enough to see that some of the cells have people in them as well. About halfway down the space he is shoved into one of the cells and the sliding cell door is slammed shut. The man then walks down the concrete hallway, his boots echoing in the space. Finally, a heavy door is slammed shut and there is nothing.

He looks around the cell, which is basically a 6-foot-by-6-foot, white room with a cot, no blankets or pillow, and a steel toilet and sink combination. He is shivering and scared. None of this makes sense. What is this place? What do they want from him? Are they going to hurt him? Kill him? These dark thoughts cause him to collapse to the floor where he silently weeps. The next thing Luis remembers is waking up on the hard floor, still naked and covered in that same white powder. He was so exhausted from his ordeal that he passed out. His eyes are puffy and red, stinging from the powder. He gets up and finds a small, hand towel on the edge of the sink and uses it to wipe the powder off his face and out of his eyes. He then pulls on a pair of white paints and a matching white shirt that must've been brought while he was unconscious. Now what? After what seems like an eternity, he musters up the courage to move to the edge of the cell and looks into the dark, hallway space. It takes him some time to work up the nerve, but finally, softly, he calls out.

"Hello."

There is nothing but silence and he waits several minutes before calling out again.

"Is anybody there?"

Again, there is nothing. Luis thinks he remembers seeing others on his way in, but he was so tired that he wonders if he imagined it.

"Please answer. I'm very afraid."

"You must be quiet," a young, female voice answers. "We are not allowed to speak."

“Where are we?”

His query is met with silence.

“Why am I here? I don’t understand.”

After a long pause, the same girl says, “I don’t know where we are. None of us do.”

“How long have you been here?”

“I don’t know,” she whispers. “But we are not allowed to talk to each other. If we do, we get punished. You have to be quiet, okay?”

“Okay,” he answers, starting to cry.

“What is your name?” the voice asks.

“Luis.”

“My name is Hannah.”

CHAPTER SIXTEEN

Rachel kneels down to talk to Lydia at face level. She wishes the examination room didn't look so stark. They only use it when members of the Legion return and on the rare occasion that new people are brought in, so normally it doesn't bother her. But with this wide-eyed, frightened little girl looking around, Rachel wishes it looked a little less antiseptic. White, concrete walls and stainless-steel counters are hardly very homey. But then again, after the life this girl has been living, a sterile, examination room probably does little to frighten her. After helping Lydia wiggle up onto the examination table, she offers her best smile to try and convey a feeling of empathy.

"Honey. Do you hurt anywhere? Does anything bother you?" Rachel asks.

Lydia, now alone in the same examining room that Clark had been in, won't make eye contact, keeping her head down. While she has developed enough trust of Rachel to be alone with her for the exam, she is still very uneasy. But knowing that Clark is just outside the room bolstered her confidence enough that she agreed to the exam.

"You know, when I was a little girl, I hated going to the doctor. My doctor was an old man and his breath smelled like coffee and cigarettes."

Lydia still doesn't look up and Rachel realizes quickly that this girl probably has no idea what coffee and cigarettes even are.

"What I remember the most about him is that he never trimmed his nose hair. He had long, gray hairs hanging out of his nose and they'd go in and out of his nostrils when he'd breathe.

Lydia tries to hide it, but Rachel sees the little girl try to hold back a faint smile.

"I used to imagine myself grabbing them and giving them a yank. I figured if I did that then maybe I wouldn't have to go see him anymore."

Lydia finally looks up, just a hint of a grin on her face. Rachel smiles back.

“It’s okay, you can tell me. Maybe I can help. Is there anything that hurts?”

Lydia slowly nods.

"Can you point to where it hurts?"

After some hesitation, she deliberately moves her hand to her mouth and points inside.

"Is it your throat?"

Lydia shakes her head no.

"Your tongue?"

Again, she communicates no.

"Is it your teeth?"

Lydia nods her head yes.

"Let me take a look, okay. Can you open your mouth?"

After looking around the room, taking in all of the equipment, she looks at Rachel with big, hopeful brown eyes and opens her mouth. As gently as she can, Rachel, aided with a tongue depressor and small flashlight, looks inside to see two teeth near the back that are rotted down to almost nothing. In fact, most of her teeth are worn down significantly. Likely a side effect from starvation as her stomach acid caused severe reflux. A few weeks of medicine, not to mention food, and this should be remedied. Fortunately, mostly she still has baby teeth.

"Okay. I see the problem. Don't you worry. We can get that fixed up for you and you won't have any pain at all."

Sitting there in her white outfit, Rachel's heart breaks for the little girl. Who knows the horror she has seen? Where are her parents? Did she speak before all this happened? She was born after it all started. She has never known anything but this miserable world. She never saw a bird fly or a horse run. Never rode a merry-go-round or had ice cream with her friends. Rachel has to fight back tears that begin to well in the corners of her eyes. She continues with the examination, trying to distract herself.

"You want to hear your own heartbeat?" she says, getting a strange look from Lydia. “See this? It’s called a stethoscope. It lets me hear your heartbeat. Would you like to hear it?”

Lydia nods her head. After finding the right spot on her chest, Rachel gently puts the earpieces into Lydia’s ears and tells her to listen. For a second, she is emotionless, then her eyes light up as she hears the constant beating of her own heart.

"That's what your heart sounds like. Pretty cool, huh?"

The little girl sits in amazement, tears beginning to stream down her face. Tears of happiness at this gift given to her by a complete stranger. She reaches out and wraps her arms around Rachel's neck, hugging her. Rachel doesn't even try to hold back her own tears, just holding this little girl for whom life just got a whole lot better.

AUDIO 3

Scientists discovered what we already knew. That the virus was not a naturally occurring illness, as markers showed it was manmade. Diplomats tried and ultimately failed to stop the crumbling relationships among countries. Soon, alliances began and tensions grew. Accusations flew and conspiracy theories were spewed from all sides.

Each day, the growing number of the infected were tearing cities and countries apart before dying, immediately replaced by newly infected humans who continued these murderous rampages. As thousands, then hundreds of thousands, then millions died each week, society completely broke down. Law enforcement became useless, and chaos spread across the globe.

The superpowers of this time were the United States, Russia and China. As it turned out, many other countries also had nuclear capability. Some countries sided with China, some with Russia, others with the Americans. In the end, as much out of fear as anything else, the final war was waged. But unlike wars of the past that lasted for years, this one was over in a flash and the result was the scorched Earth and dark skies that now remain.

While all the countries blamed one another, none were actually to blame. It was us. A nation-less collective with unfinished business. A long-forgotten people with an agenda that had to be satisfied. The virus we unleashed on the world was designed to kill everybody, but it didn't. As with anything, we knew there would be exceptions. The nuclear response was also expected and in the case that anybody survived the virus, it would ultimately finish the job.

While nations spent billions of dollars creating defense programs to monitor the skies and protect themselves from attack, in reality, it was all a waste. For years, nations across the world had infiltrated foreign lands, constructing nuclear weapons that would never need to be launched because they were built and hidden in strategic locations across the globe. At that point, when the war started and the first was detonated, retaliation was immediate as ground detonations ensued across the world. In a matter of minutes, everything was destroyed and the skies went dark.

Even then, with all the horror, I still foolishly believed in what we were doing. I was wrong. We all were.

CHAPTER SEVENTEEN

Following another round of decontamination showers, and more time in the purple lighted room, Lydia and Clark follow Rachel into a different room, this one requiring not only a hand scan but also a retinal scan from Rachel. Inside a guard is stationed. He pulls the door shut, pushes a few buttons on a console and an eerie sliding sound is followed by a heavy click as the door is secured.

The security inside this facility seems unending but knowing what the world is like outside, Clark absolutely understands its necessity.

The soldier then slides past Lydia, Clark and Rachel, bends down a little, puts his eyes up against a pair of tubes on the wall and waits while a double-retina scan is done. Finally, an audible click is heard and the door opens and they enter a room where three men are sitting at a white table, in an all-white room.

"Clark. Lydia. I'd like to introduce you. This is Conrad Biehn, Stephan Hoffman and Tod Heilen, they are the three top ranking administrators of this facility," Rachel says.

"How do you do Dr. Higgenbothum?" says Conrad, a man in his early 50s with white hair and thick-framed bifocals that frame his jovial face. He, Tod and Stephan are dressed in blue pants, with white button-down shirts and matching blue ties.

"Nice to meet you," Clark says with a handshake. "You have an amazing facility here."

"Well thank you. But in reality, you've not seen much of it."

"To us, it's a paradise."

"Good. We are glad you have been comfortable. I trust that Rachel has taken care of any and all of your needs," says Stephan, a small man of roughly the same age as Conrad, but with sandy brown hair and delicate features.

"Yes, she has been great. I am still kind of in shock with everything. It's so clean and warm in here compared to out there."

"I imagine you have many questions." Conrad says as he moves from behind the table and walks over to Lydia, taking a knee on the concrete floor. "And what is your name?"

"Her name is Lydia," Clark says. "She doesn't talk."

"I see," Conrad says with a grandfatherly smile. "Well, you are a very lovely young lady."

Lydia just looks down at her feet, her face full of fear. She has never known anything but treachery and pain. This strange man now addressing her causes her to vibrate with anxiety.

"Young lady, there is nothing for you to be afraid of," Conrad says as he gently lifts her face by the chin and then brushes her thick, black hair behind her ear. "We are friends. We want to be your friends, too."

Conrad gets back to his feet and motions for Clark and Rachel to take a seat as he moves back around the table to his seat. Clark and Rachel take a seat while the guard stands quietly in the corner. Lydia crawls up and sits on Clark's lap.

"This place is amazing. Who runs it? How did this place come into being? And, not that I'm complaining, why have we been brought here?" Clark asks in a tone that conveys gratitude.

"All great questions," Conrad says. "I can only imagine what you've been through and how this place must be quite difficult to believe."

"I keep waiting to wake up," Clark says, eliciting a laugh from everybody in the room.

"When the virus mutated and people became unhinged, tensions around the world grew about whose fault it was. It was just a matter of time before we got to this point," Conrad says with serious eyes as he folds his hands and places them on the table. "Our world was facing extinction in the wake of a war such as this world had never seen before. It was inevitable."

Clark is quiet as he already knows most of this. He lived through it. After a pause, Stephan picks up the story.

"Many years ago, construction on this facility began in case of some global calamity. It took decades to complete. You see Dr. Higgenbothum, when tensions rose and the war looked imminent, we and a small contingent of others came here for sanctuary. A small skeleton crew had lived here for many years, working in monthly shifts, preparing for the end. Before this nuclear winter is over, nothing will remain outside of this place. We have created a safe haven for mankind so that one day, when the skies clear, we can start again."

"Start again?" Clarks asks, having long ago given up any hope for the future of the Earth.

"Yes. When we emerge from the ground like hibernating animals after a long winter slumber," says Tod, who is slighter taller than Conrad and Stephan. "We have carefully planned for that day. A day when this world will be reborn."

Tod looks to be in his early 50s, with dark, brown hair, grayish-blue eyes, thin lips and a dark beard and moustache. He wears shaggy, shoulder-length hair that Stephan and Conrad have repeatedly requested that he trim, not feeling the look is dignified.

Conrad picks up the story.

"We have been preparing for the time when we will reclaim the Earth and ... start over."

"This is incredible. Are there other places like this?" Clark wonders out loud.

"It is doubtful," Stephan says. "Even governments who had fallout shelters that they thought were secret have likely been destroyed. The sheer cost of this place was great. It nearly didn't get built because even billionaires had trepidation about the massive cost involved. Contractors were paid ten times their usual wage but had to agree to be brought here in windowless vehicles for weeks on end, having no idea where they were or what they were actually building. It was quite an undertaking, with nobody seeing the entire facility."

"The entire facility?" Clark asks.

"What you have seen so far is just a fraction," Conrad says. "There is so much more for you to see, that is, if you are interested."

"I am very interested. But why us?"

"Mason is a recruiter of sorts," Stephan says. "You see, when we built this facility, we tried to take every variable into account. The people who were asked to live here included doctors, scientists, engineers, architects, teachers and much more. The top people in their fields. These are people who would provide the expertise in our underground society here as well as jumpstarting our civilization when we leave."

“I still don’t understand.”

"We needed another physician. Somebody with your pedigree," Conrad interjects.

"How could you know anything about me? I could be a quack."

"Top of your class at Yale, a specialist in hematology, several impressive papers published on new, cutting-edge ways to combat diseases at the cellular level."

"How could you possibly know that?" Clark says.

"Mason told us," Conrad says.

"Huh?"

"We have the capability of communicating over short distances with a technology that is similar to what used to amount to texting on cell phones,"

Stephan says. “He told us who you are and we have archives of information that we were able to pull up on you. Quite impressive."

"I am at a loss for words."

“After researching you, we were pleasantly surprised by your accomplishments,” Stephan says. “For somebody so young, you accumulated some impressive credentials. But it was your work in the field of genetics, including two papers you published in the New England Journal of Medicine that really got our attention. You were lauded for theories that at one time were thought to be medical impossibilities.”

“That was a long time ago. I’m not sure what help I can be.”

“You’re too modest,” Tod says. “Genius doesn’t simply disappear.”

“So, what is it you would ask of me?”

“To continue your work,” Conrad says with a friendly smile. “We have resources here that are quite impressive. Your research was groundbreaking. It still can be. Like everybody here, you will have purpose to help better our community.”

“Community?”

Stephan, Tod and Conrad all laugh with joy at the question as they know that Clark is about to be stunned.

"The question is this. Do you wish to join us? If you do, you will have to stay until it is safe to go up top. It may be another 10 or 15 years. Nobody can be sure."

"So, my choice is to be safe here, with good food and nobody trying to kill us, or to go take our chances out there?"

"Yes. That is pretty much the choice," Tod says with a warm smile and jovial chuckle at Clark’s sarcastic query.

Considering that every day for as long as he can remember, Clark half expected to die. Day after day, the very real threat of death hung over he and Lydia. To now have this gift bestowed upon them is hard to quantify.

Clark looks at Lydia and says "so whatta ya think kid?"

She smiles at him and nods her head.

Clark slowly looks at everybody in the room and then, with a smile says, "Where do we sign up?"

CHAPTER EIGHTEEN

With Conrad leading the way, Rachel, Clark and Lydia navigate several short hallways and two more airlocks before entering a long corridor that is painted bright yellow. It's the first color he can remember seeing in a longtime as everything outside was dank, dirty and gray. At the end of the hallway, they come to a door where Conrad must crouch down for another retinal scan. The door latch promptly pops and Conrad puts his hand on the door handle and then turns to Clark with a smile.

"Are you ready for your lives to change?"

Conrad slowly pulls the door open, keeping his eyes on Clark and Lydia. It's very rare to get new people and he loves to watch their faces the first time they see it. The feeling of superiority this gives Conrad is hard to quantify. He loves the feeling it gives him to alter their destiny in such an amazing manner, which gives him a nearly God-like quality that he finds intoxicating.

As if in a fog, still holding Lydia's hand, Clark walks through the opening, his mouth hanging open with wonderment at this amazing place. Conrad shuts the door behind them, it automatically bolting shut. Conrad then walks out in front of them, slowly turning and pausing for dramatic effect. They are outside. But how can this be?

"I'd like to formally welcome you to the Ark," Conrad says.

If he didn't know any better, Clark would think he was standing on a sidewalk in a small Midwest town. The streets and sidewalks are full of bustling people milling about, looking as if they are out running errands. There are rows of buildings on both sides, with stores and what look to be small businesses on the bottom. A seamstress, a dentist, an optometrist, a coffee house, several restaurants, a large church, complete with steeple and cross, even a shoe store. The buildings, which are brick colonials in style, are perfectly manicured, not so much as a chip in the paint. Not a gum wrapper or cigarette butt can be found on the ground. As amazing as this giant, underground town is, the sky is the true wonder of this place.

"What do you think?" Conrad asks.

"How can this be?" Clark says, pointing to the blue sky with soft, billowy clouds gently rolling along, occasionally hiding the sun before revealing its golden glow.

"Ah yes. Pretty spectacular isn't it," Conrad says. "After the Ark was built, we felt something was missing. As awesome as the architecture is, a 120-foot-high, dank, domed ceiling just wouldn't do. We brought in the top special effects team in the world at the time. Using projectors and state-of-the-art technology, they were able to create the sky that you see today."

"Incredible," Clark utters.

"It goes on a 24-hour cycle," Conrad offers. "Creating day and night. It helps the citizens with a sense of normalcy. We have spectacular sunrises and sunsets, rainbows, moon phases at night, even meteor showers. The temperature even drops slightly in the evening when the sun goes down. After you are here for a while, at times, you will even forget that you are living underground."

“Don’t try to figure it all out right away,” Rachel says, obviously recognizing that Clark’s senses are starting to overload. “You will be surprised how quickly you will adjust.

Clark gets that woozy feeling again, getting the sensation that he already saw this. In only lasts a few seconds, and then it is gone.

With a nod of the head in agreement at Rachel’s wise words, Conrad begins walking, urging the others to follow. They begin strolling down the street, seeing people of all ages, wearing a variety of different clothing, going about their business. A woman in a white apron delivers coffee mugs to a young couple sitting in a small, outdoor cafe. Another man sits quietly in a little alcove, painting on an easel while a few onlookers watch his progress. A large man with thick forearms and a chef's hat laughs heartily as he talks to two men who are enjoying some food. A tall woman in a neatly, tailored dress is re-arranging two mannequins in stylish clothing in a storefront.

There are a few side streets in the distance as well, Clark quickly realizing that there is much more than just this one thoroughfare.

"How big is this place?" Clark asks, overwhelmed by all he is seeing.

"The town itself is 600 meters long and 325 meters wide," Conrad rattles off the measurements with robotic efficiency. "Basically, there is Main Street, which we are on, and then there are four other streets, two on either side of us. Essentially, we have five streets all running parallel to each other, like a city grid, with side streets connecting them. We also have a park, a swimming pool, climbing walls, a running track, a sports arena and many other wonderful amenities.

On occasion, Conrad or Rachel return a wave from somebody, but nobody stops them, obviously aware that new arrivals need to some time to acclimate. There are people of all ages milling about, in clean clothes with rosy complexions, a far cry from the rags that the emaciated people on the outside wear.

A middle-aged man with a thick, dark moustache, bushy eyebrows, and graying hair standing in front of a storefront smiles when he sees the two new arrivals, walking like tourists, their eyes taking in everything. He disappears for a moment before abruptly re-emerging a few seconds later with a candy apple in his hand. He walks out onto the sidewalk.

"Good afternoon, Lou," Conrad says with a jovial tone and a pat on the back.

"Hello," he says with a big, toothy grin.

"What have you got there?" Rachel says with a knowing smile.

"Just a little gift for this young lady here ... that is ... if it's alright," he says, looking to Clark.

"Sure," Clark says, his eyes beaming as he watches Lydia's brown eyes get wide.

Lou takes a knee right in front of Lydia and extends the treat to her.

"Go ahead sweetheart. Try it. I just made it this morning. I'll bet you have never had anything so tasty."

Lydia looks up to Clark who smiles and nods his head to her. After a few seconds of hesitation, she accepts the candy apple, looking at it kind of perplexed.

"Well. Go ahead. Bite into it. You don't want to hurt my feelings, do you?"

Lydia spins it a few times, looking for just the right spot and then, after inspecting it thoroughly, she takes a big, healthy bite. Her eyes light up when the burst of flavor hits her pallet. Never in her life has she tasted something so glorious. Before she can even stop herself, she takes three more quick bites, the juices dripping down her chin.

"I'd say she likes it Lou," Rachel says with a laugh.

"Apples. How in the world do you have fresh apples?" Clark asks.

"We grow them, of course," Conrad says proudly.

"How?"

"We have a hydroponics facility here," Conrad says. "I can arrange a tour of it later if you wish. Outside of this town, we have numerous corridors full of food wonders you can't even begin to imagine.

"I would like that very much."

"You must stop by once you get settled," Lou says. "I am preparing some special treats this week that you must try."

"Absolutely," Clarks says, shaking hands with the gregarious man who is obviously a chef of some sort.

Stephan and Tod excuse themselves, while Conrad continues the tour, moving slowly through the town, exploring this amazing subterranean world.

"Everybody seems pretty busy in one way or another," Clark says as he points to a barber shop that is full of men laughing and chatting while awaiting their turn in the chair. While Clark has already shaved off his scraggly beard, his long hair is in need of some attention.

"Of course. Everybody here has duties to attend to," Conrad says. "Something as simple as sweeping the street or serving a warm beverage is pivotal. It is key to keeping our civilization going, preserving a sense of normalcy until we can emerge in the world again. Not only does it make our community run better, but it gives everybody a sense of purpose. A reason to get up each day."

"So, everybody has a job?"

"Well. Yes. Every adult has a designation," Conrad says.

"What about me?"

"When you are ready, your skills will be a tremendous asset here. That is, if you are interested." Rachel says.

"How?"

"At the hospital, of course," Conrad says with a grin.

"You have a hospital?"

"Of course. Every good town needs a hospital," he says with pride in his voice.

CHAPTER NINETEEN

They arrive at the hospital and after saying their good-byes to Rachel, who has to get to work for her shift, Conrad continues the tour with Clark and Lydia. Conrad decides to give them a quick walk through. Normally he wouldn't tour the hospital with them but considering that it's been quite a while since they've had a new doctor in town, Conrad wants to show Clark the facility.

The three-story structure is located at the far end of the town, complete with an emergency entrance. It is like a miniature version of the giant hospital buildings that Clark remembers. The bottom floor includes a waiting room, receptionist desk, nurses and doctors in scrubs moving about, examination rooms, a radiology department and even an MRI machine. There are also two, small operating rooms.

The second floor is for in-patients, mostly empty except for two patients. There is a man recovering from surgery on a ruptured Achilles tendon he suffered while playing Squash, and there is one child who had his tonsils removed. Both are waited on hand and foot. Not only do they receive round-the-clock care from the doctors and nurses, but also a whole host of others who staff the hospital in a variety of capacities.

The third floor contains a few small offices for the doctors, a physical therapy room staffed with two PTs helping one middle-aged man who is dealing with a shoulder issue, and an impressive lab with state-of-the-art equipment.

"This is called the Becker-Mueller Hospital, named after the late Dr. Arthur Becker and Fredrich Mueller. Their donations and expertise made this place possible."

“How many people can live here?” Clark asks.

"In the Ark? It can house up to 1,200 people comfortably."

"So, 1,200 people live here?"

"Oh goodness no. We currently, including our two newest citizens, have 729 people who reside here. So, as you can see, the staff at the hospital always greatly outnumbers the patients. But still, it gives everybody something to do. Without having a purpose, living underground could get difficult for some people."

"If you are overstaffed, why are you interested in me? Why bring me in from the outside ... not that I'm complaining."

"Of course. A very fair question. While we do have doctors, nurses, radiologists, physicians' assistants, physical therapists, urologists, gynecologists and other specialists, your area of expertise is something we are in need of."

"What? Hematology?" Clarks asks.

"Yes. Particularly your concentrated area of hemoglobinopathies."

"Wow. You guys really do your homework."

"I understand that you worked under Dr. Malcolm Ford, who was doing cutting edge work in that field, including some promising work with Beta-thalassemia."

"Yes. Dr. Ford was a genius. I learned a lot from him."

"Well, like any small town, people here have a medley of medical needs."

"You don't have a hematologist here?"

"We did. Actually, Dr. Carlson wore a lot of hats here. A brilliant man. Hematology was just one area of expertise. He was of advanced age. Actually, he was among the oldest people here. But he was in good health so it was shocking when we lost him unexpectedly."

"Oh. I see."

"We tried to plan for everything, but as you can imagine, to be prepared for every problem that arises was an impossibility."

"Which is why Mason does what he does?" Clark says.

"Yes. There are several areas that we are … 'recruiting' for if you want to call it that. As you can see, we were very happy when Mason found you."

"Not as happy as I am." Clark says with a laugh.

"I think you will discover that the Ark has all the comforts of home."

"I still have a tough time believing that all of this exists. It's amazing."

"And there is so much more."

"It's a wonder."

"So. What do you two say? Would you like to see your apartment?"

"Apartment?"

"Yes. We have a strict policy against homelessness here," Conrad says with a smile. "Everybody gets their own place. Somewhere to call home. I assume Lydia will be staying with you?"

"Yes," Clark answers firmly.

"Of course."

CHAPTER TWENTY

The stroll from the hospital is still overwhelming as the architecture and attention to detail is incredible. Even the two story, six-room schoolhouse matches the town. Even the large, bronze school bell out front has been aged to look like it has been there for centuries.

They turn down the street at the end of the town, stopping in front of a structure with a gold exterior highlighted by burnt red accents. It's a charming building, a four-story brick design. Outside, some children are playing Double Dutch, smiles stretched across their faces. All the children are too young to have ever known the outside world, adjusting easily to life underground was much easier for them than the adults as they've never known any different.

"Seeing kids playing is incredible," Clark remarks. "That's something I never thought I'd see again."

"Yes. Being that it is Saturday, the Ark is full of kids enjoying the weekend. Children here love weekends, holidays and summer vacation, just like they used to before it all happened."

Clark smiles, having long ago forgotten about different days of the week, not to mention holidays, birthdays and other dates. On the outside, none of that has held any meaning for a long time.

"Do you see them, Lydia?" Conrad says, moving toward Lydia and stroking her thick, dark, curly hair. "There are many, many children here. I think you are going to make some good friends."

Lydia has the urge to pull away, but isn't sure if she should, so she stands quietly, looking at the ground until they begin walking again.

After entering a set of double doors, Conrad leads Lydia and Clark up a narrow, but intricately designed staircase to the second floor where they stroll to the end of the hall. There, Conrad removes a key from his pocket, unlocks the brown, wooden door and opens it. After allowing Lydia and Clark to enter, he follows. The apartment is decorated nicely, painted in a warm, yellow with light, brown carpeting throughout. There are also a few copies of framed Carl Spitzweg reprints on the walls. The main living room, while small, has a green sofa and two, brown straight-back chairs. There are two small bedrooms with dressers and single beds in each, as well as a bathroom with a toilet, small sink and even a corner shower.

"Each unit has its own electric, mini hot water tank," Conrad says proudly. "Usually, it provides enough hot water for about 15 minutes in the shower before it starts to get cold. However, it does refill quickly, about 30 minutes or so and it is ready to use again."

"Our own hot shower?" Clark says in amazement.

"And if you need anything fixed or worked on, anything at all, simply go down to the lobby and write your room number and description of your problem on the chalkboard and it will be fixed promptly by somebody from our maintenance department."

"How do I pay them?"

"Money does not exist here," Conrad says with a hearty chuckle. "Everybody here works for the good of the society."

"Like communism."

"Well. Yes. I guess you could call it that. On the outside, communism didn't always work well because the people who lived in communist nations knew that neighboring countries didn't practice it. I suppose there was always that envy and greed. The 'I want to have more' mentality. That doesn't exist here because there are no neighbors to be envious of because everybody is given the same accommodations. The people here see how well this way of living works. Greed does not exist and would not be tolerated."

"It's hard for me to get used to the idea of just getting something for nothing," Clark asks.

"It's not for nothing. Every adult contributes to our society. You, for instance, can help provide healthcare to our citizens here. All of this is your payment. Everybody else is the same."

"Food, clothing, anything?"

"Yes. Every citizen is allotted three meals a day as well as some special items such as coffee, tea and, yes, even treats. You may also order clothing, shoes and other necessities. Setup a dentist appointment, maybe get a haircut."

"What about Lydia? What will she do while I am at the hospital?"

"School, of course."

"School?"

"We have a fine school, complete with teachers, administrators, child psychologists and more. After all, these children are the future of our civilization."

"I don't know if she is ready for that, yet."

"I think you will be surprised. Children are incredibly resilient," Conrad says with an almost dismissing wave of the hand that strikes Clark as strange.

"But she doesn't talk."

"Oh. That's okay," Conrad says with a wink at Lydia as he gently strokes her cheek. "Sometimes I myself don't feel like talking either. Nothing wrong with listening, is there honey?"

Lydia subconsciously turns away from him subtly, a furrowed brow the only evidence that she disliked Conrad's touch.

"Anything you need, within reason, can probably be accommodated," Conrad continues, offering another big smile.

"I'm speechless," Clark says.

"I totally understand. I am going to leave you to get situated. Then, feel free to explore your new town. Stop and get a bite to eat. Order some new clothes. Take in a movie if you like."

"You have a movie theatre?"

"Of course," Conrad says with jubilation in his voice. "The apartments have no televisions because we don't want people to just sit at home watching TV. We'd rather that people be out, after all, that's all part of having a thriving community. But people still like to get lost in a good film. There is a theatre just two blocks from here with many favorite movies. I believe one of the showings later today is a cartoon. Peter Pan, I think."

"What then?"

"There is no hurry. Simply take some time to get used to life here. I will stop by in a few days to see how you are getting along."

"What time? What if we aren't here?"

Conrad laughs again. "It's a small town, I'm sure I will run into you soon."

CHAPTER TWENTY-ONE

Mark Gibbenhofer, known to everybody as "Gibby," is 23 years old, and quite a physical specimen. Standing 6-feet-4 with short, blonde hair and possessing a chiseled physique, he looks imposing as he circles to his right. Other than Mason, Gibby is the most gifted physical member of the Legion. His hand-to-hand skills are vast and he's an expert marksman. Wearing beige cargo pants and no shirt or shoes, he carefully moves across the blue, padded floor. While known amongst the other members of the Legion for his aggressiveness, he is being uncharacteristically methodical.

"He's stalling," somebody shouts, eliciting a couple of laughs from the small group of Legion members at this training session.

Mason, dressed identically to Gibby, has a slight smile on his face as he too moves to his right. Unlike Gibby, Mason has a multitude of scars on his torso as he has spent much more time in the field, something Gibby has only begun to do. Other than Rachel, and the late Dr. Ben Carlson, Gibby is the only other person he trusts. When Gibby was just a prospective candidate, Mason took an interest in the young man, spending countless hours tutoring him in all facets of what it takes to be in the Legion, including endless hand-to-hand combat sessions. In fact, it was Mason's efforts over many years that have helped transform Gibby into the man he has become, ultimately earning him a spot of the team. As the youngest and newest member of the Legion, Gibby looks to Mason, who is in his mid-30s, as almost a big brother of sorts. And like any younger brother, he wants nothing more than to best his mentor and prove himself.

"This is my day, Mason," Gibby says with a jovial tone.

"You might be right."

"I've been practicing."

"Me too," Mason says, getting a laugh from the men watching, knowing that his practice was on the outside, far different from the safe confines of this padded, warm room.

This group is known simply as the Legion, who have been trained since they were infants for the singular purpose of protecting and serving the Ark. The other two are out on missions, as all eight are rarely together at one time. There used to be 12, but over the years, some went out into the wastelands and never returned. Already, there are six young prospects of varying ages who undergo ongoing training with hopes of one day becoming part of the Legion, which is like royalty among the inhabitants of the Ark. In fact, in addition to duties outside of the Ark, part of the Legion's purpose is in protecting the residents and keeping order. Although, there is rarely any reason for them to discipline the citizens of this underground paradise and conflicts are quite rare.

"You look tired," Gibby says.

"Yep. Exhausted," Mason retorts with a smile.

After a few more verbal barbs between the two combatants, Gibby gets jumpy and lunges forward, taking a hard slash with his weapon, easily evaded by Mason who smiles. Again, Gibby attacks, this time with a stabbing motion, drawing nothing but air. A few cheers and jeers come from the other four men, all bare-chested, bare-footed and wearing the same issued pants.

Like Mason, these men were handpicked and raised to be the ultimate soldiers. They obey their commanding officers without question, each ready to give his life for the cause. While Mason trusts some more than others, the one thing he knows is that these men will follow orders without question. Other than himself, only Gibby has ever shown to have any sort of moral code. The rest, who have been trained to act like upstanding citizens when in social situations, have a darkness that Mason can feel. For that reason, Mason interacts with them, but doesn't necessarily trust each of them. He has seen enough to know that most of them are cold-blooded killers, something he chooses not to be.

While Mason is the recognized alpha, like a pack of wolves, these highly trained, aggressive soldiers are always looking for the opportunity to lead the pack. But since they were young, Mason has always been the best, having proven it over and over. So, for now, he is recognized as the top dog of the Legion.

Mason moves quickly to his right raising his blade in his right hand. Gibby raises his weapon to block the knife attack and receives a thunderous Muy Thai kick to the outside of his right thigh, nearly collapsing his leg.

"Always watch all four limbs of your opponent."

"Screw off," Gibby says, getting a laugh from the men.

Smiling, like the friendliest of assassins, Mason expertly slashes with his weapon, leaving a crimson-colored line along Gibby's forearm while simultaneously pounding the outside of the other thigh with another kick. Mason continues this calculated battle, attacking high and then blasting the legs of his large opponent. Gibby's thighs are already in the beginning stages of cramping from this battle, his motion now awkward and unbalanced. He is starting to stagger around, his legs betraying him.

Mason has always liked Gibby and for that reason, has been taking it easy on him so far. Some of the other members of the Legion are not nearly as genuine and trustworthy, and for that reason, in similar situations, Mason rarely holds back. He knows the importance of establishing his dominance with them as he doesn't want any of them to believe they have a chance. He needs to convey invincibility. But even now, with Mason not choosing to utilize his full arsenal, the ending is clear.

"It's all over but the crying," one man shouts.

Gibby loses his composure, as Mason knew he would, bull rushing in a desperate attempt to snatch victory from the jaws of defeat. Patience has always been his weakness, something Mason continues to work on with him. Mason falls to his back, grabbing the wrist of his attacker in one hand, his feet finding the chest of Gibby and easily flipping him into the air where he lands on his back, the wind momentarily leaving him. Mason then leaps to his feet in a flash where he waits for his struggling opponent to get to off the mat.

Gibby slowly gets to his knees, taking in deep breaths, finally making it to his feet.

There is no need to prolong the agony any longer as Mason moves in for the kill. He blocks two front kicks from Gibby, slashing with his weapon across the stomach, leaving a trail of red from the strike. Gibby tries a hard left hook but is blocked as Mason carves the winning blow right across the throat of his opponent, who falls to his back.

"Your reign is over Gibby," somebody shouts, announcing the fact that Gibby has not lost since Mason has been gone.

"Dammit!" Gibby growls.

Mason goes over, extends a hand and helps his opponent to his feet.

"Good job."

"Not good enough," Gibby says with a sheepish smile.

"Everybody loses sometimes,"

"Except you."

"Yeah. Except for me," Mason says with a smile.

Gibby accepts a towel from one of the other Legion members and wipes off the paint that oozes from the plastic training blades to indicate a strike.

Nobody expected Mason to be back in the training facility so soon after his mission, but to him, there is nowhere else he would rather be. After all, having been in training since as far back as he can remember, he doesn't know any other way to live.

The members of the Legion are a team when in the Ark, but each are sent on missions individually and are sworn to secrecy. Each has a different objective, and none will ever discuss it.

They tease and joke around but it's all an act. An elaborate performance for when they are in the Ark. Just part of the training. Their responses socially are every bit as calculated as their fighting styles.

It particularly bothers Mason because he feels like a robot being switched on and off, something that has always troubled him. In the same way he feels nothing when he kills somebody, he also feels nothing when verbally sparring in a playful manner with the guys or when he flirts with one of the female residents of the town. He's like an autonomous creation, unable to break free of his programming.

The trainers realized early on that creating a killer without any balance would be a recipe for disaster. So social protocols were introduced simultaneously with grueling training. Through study, role-playing, hypnosis and behavior modification, the men can switch from assassin to jovial in a flash. For this reason, Mason isn't sure who he actually is. Where does the charade end and he begin? Perhaps that's why he refuses to kill a retreating foe and is known to bring in strays to the dismay of his superiors. It's something he, and he alone, decides.

AUDIO 4

I never really liked the name "The Ark." Being a man of science, I never put much stock in biblical references. The notion of a magic man living above the clouds, one who is responsible for everybody and everything always seemed ludicrous to me. I don't like to guess; I seek hard data and results. The Ark refers to a man from the bible named Noah who saved the world by loading people and two of every animal into a boat to avoid a cataclysmic flood. I argued against such a spectacular facility being named off a fairytale, but that's what they wanted to call it. Considering that many of the men who created the Ark are God-fearing people, I was in the minority as an atheist. A short-sighted group with no vision of their own was how I used to feel about it. But in reality, what they chose to call it is largely inconsequential.

The plan for it was originally conceived in the late 1930s but actual construction didn't begin until many decades later. It took more than 30 years to complete and even I, who have the top clearances available to anybody that is not part of the council, have not seen it all or know how far it goes. What I can tell you is that it is much larger than anybody thinks. There are levels to this facility that only a choice few have ever seen and that hold deadly secrets.

Originally, I was very proud of this accomplishment and to be part of this movement. From my earliest days, I was groomed for this, and I bought into this movement. But I have become awakened to treachery that I never would have thought possible. Suddenly I was questioning everything I thought I knew. That's because I believe now that I and countless others have built our lives around deceit. I once pompously felt that I was one of the brightest minds in my field. Now, I feel like an absolute fool. Like some sort of uneducated rube who got taken by some carnival conman.

The Ark was built mostly in secret and for any workers who were brought here basically blindfolded, were told that it was a bunker created in case of some natural calamity. Only a handful of trusted people ever knew its true purpose.

You and the others who reside here were handpicked for a very specific purpose. I was raised from my earliest days to support the cause. A purpose I wholeheartedly believed in until I learned the truth. Now I realize that my pompousness is to blame for all that followed. My yearning to be superior, ignoring any other variable that existed outside of science, proved to be my biggest failing.

Now, all I feel is shame at my role in all that is terrible in this world.

CHAPTER TWENTY-TWO

Lydia's eyes light up as she watches the group of kids on the adventure of a lifetime. The colorful scenery, the musical soundtrack, the funny voices of characters, it's all so amazing. Flying above the lighted city, off to Never Never Land, it's like getting lost in a completely different world. Even Captain Hook, who is supposed to be the evil character in the story, looks friendly to her. But then again, after seeing true evil, these child-friendly animations are hard-pressed to frighten her.

The entire experience is unlike anything she could have ever imagined. She has never even seen a television, at least not one that isn't smashed on the ground with all of the other debris from a once thriving world that has been demolished. Here, in this small but beautifully kept movie theater, its red-curtained walls, comfortable, padded seats and climate-controlled interior, it is the happiest she has ever been.

"Don't forget this," Clarks whispers as he hands her a red and white container. "It's kind of ... part of the experience."

The scent of the warm butter takes Clark back to his childhood when he and his family would go to the movies once a month. He urges her to give it a try. She smiles and digs her hand into the plastic container, pulling out a handful of the fluffy, yellow popcorn and pops it in her mouth, the flavors exploding. Her eyes get big and she looks up to Clark, a buttery smile making his heart melt. She never imagined any food could be so wonderful.

Clark too is mesmerized by the experience. From the bow-tied staff that works the theater, to the snack bar, complete with a variety of treats, Clark has actually been starting to relax a little, the tension dissolving from his shoulders. The theater, which has about 75 seats, is less than half full, many in the audience are giggling children. The sheer normalness of it all almost brings

Clark to tears. The joy on Lydia's innocent face is something he never imagined he would ever get to see.

The small, dim lights on the wall flash bright for an instant, then go back to normal. Clark notices, but Lydia is entranced in the film, oblivious to everything except the film.

As Wendy and Peter fly above the island, a huge smile stretches across Lydia's face. This magical realm that she and Clark have been brought to is unlike any place she has ever known. Until a few days ago, she knew no other existence but the one she endured in that horrible place.

She leans her head on Clark's shoulder, plunging her hand into the container of popcorn and shoveling more of this delicious, magical food into her mouth.

"Happy," she says in an unnatural voice, kind of froggy.

"What? What did you say?" Clark says with shock on his face having never heard her utter a word before.

"Happy!" she says again, this time her throat a little looser, the words sounding more like that of a little girl.

Clark puts his arms around her, hugging her tightly.

"Me too, Lydia. Me too."

-

More than 100 hundred feet below the town, three men in hardhats and white overalls must shout to be heard over the deafening rush of water. Positioned on steel catwalks above the massive, underwater river, the men are installing the last piece to the new turbine, fastening the final arm onto the overhanging apparatus where it can be incorporated into the system.

Stephan has been sent to check the progress of the project, something he is uneasy about. He, Conrad and Tod all share these types of duties, and Stephan hates coming down here, largely because he is terrified of water.

Having been sheltered as a child and not very adventurous, he never learned to swim.

Here, in this massive underwater cavern, is the lifeblood of the Ark. This geological wonder, a mammoth subterranean river that is nearly 70 yards wide and 20 yards deep, provides drinking and bathing water for the entire town thanks to a network of pipes, filters and plumbing. Five massive turbines provide the electricity for all of the Ark's needs. This river is the reason the Ark was built where it is.

After carefully climbing a set of metal stairs and cautiously making his way across one of the catwalks, Stephan addresses the workers.

"How are we doing?" he asks the man closest to him.

"Hello sir. We are doing great. We are ready to test it."

"Very good."

"This additional turbine should add 15-percent to our current power output."

"Excellent. Please, proceed," Stephan says nervously, very uneasy on the catwalk and wanting to move this along.

With construction nearly complete on an additional hydroponics bay, this new turbine should provide the necessary power.

After a few more moments pass and the workers double-check to make sure everything is working properly, one of the men moves over to the far wall, holds up his hands and crosses his fingers with a smile, and then throws a lever which slowly lowers the large, steel paddlewheel into the water. In a matter of seconds, its internal parts begin spinning furiously. After about 30 seconds, the man over by the wall reads a gauge and then smiles, giving a thumbs up as the newest turbine is already sending mega-doses of electricity into the system. He then quickly shuts off the feed to the system to keep from blowing any circuits until modifications can be made to handle the extra power.

Stephan is pleased, but has already begun retreating from the catwalk, which is now shaking. His thoughts of falling into the rushing water and swept away into that dark cavern is terrifying.

"It's okay sir," one of the other man shouts to be heard above the noise. "The shaking is totally normal."

"Of course," Stephan says, forcing a smile. "I will report on the success. Good work gentlemen."

Stephan doesn’t want to appear weak, so he nods to them and moves on with a death grip on the railing, down the stairs and quickly exits the cavern, happy to be back on solid ground.

CHAPTER TWENTY-THREE

At the edge of town, a small park has been created and is a favorite place for many to end their day. There are benches, a gazebo, swings, a jungle gym and a large, open area the size of a Little League baseball field, complete with synthetic grass. Many of the children are running around, throwing Frisbees and playing tag. The adults on hand are either making small talk or trying to corral their children. It's a popular gathering place for families to congregate after work and school.

Clark and Lydia have taken a seat on one of the ornate, white, wooden park benches. Both are mesmerized, looking over a fence at the rolling hills and a sky with brilliant hues of purple and orange as the sun sets over a breathtaking horizon. Clark is still awestruck by this amazing technology that has transformed a barren wall into a glimpse of the world he used to know, one that the inhabitants of this place are keeping alive for their re-emergence.

"Beautiful, isn't it?"

"What? I mean yes, it is." Clark says, startled by the striking young, blonde woman who has knelt beside him.

"I love coming here to watch these sunsets. Do you know that no two are the same? Not ever." she says, smiling as much with her blue eyes as with her perfect, white teeth.

Clark can't get over how nice everybody's teeth are here. In fact, he had his first dental appointment and will require many sessions, including addressing seven cavities and likely a root canal. That's what happens when you don't have the opportunity to brush your teeth for years.

"Really?" Clark says.

"The program is ever evolving. Different colors, rates of descent, stars emerge at different times of the evening."

"Remarkable."

“The constellations in the night sky run on an alga rhythm that mimics exactly what the actual night sky looks like. That is, if the clouds were gone and the sky could be seen.”

“Incredible.”

"Listen to me. Making something so beautiful sound like a computer program, which it is, but still. I apologize."

"No need to apologize. I find it all fascinating," Clark says, absently running his hand through his freshly cut hair, still getting used to the fact that his long, mangy hair is now gone.

"Where are my manners? My name is Sophia. I haven't seen you two before."

"Oh. I am Clark. Clark Higgenbothum. And this is Lydia."

"Nice to meet you Lydia ... Clark Clark," she says with a joking smile. "New arrivals I take it?"

"Yes. We are."

"So. She is your daughter?"

"Yes. I mean, not biologically. But you know."

"I see," she says. "Well, it is very nice to meet you both. You are just adorable," she says with a smile at Lydia. "And look at those big, beautiful eyes."

"Thank you," Clark answers, actually finding himself flirting. "I have my father's eyes, but he let me pick my own nose."

Sophia breaks into a hard chuckle, contagious but not annoying. Clark looks at Lydia and winks, forcing her to cover her mouth and giggle, too.

"I was talking to Lydia, but I guess your eyes are pretty, too."

"Well, thank you." Clark says.

The three sit silently for a moment or two, watching as the sun completely disappears behind a distant mountain range, the colors exploding into the sky as a rogue shooting star streaks across the horizon.

“So how are you two adjusting?” Sophia asks.

“Very well, thank you. Lydia got to see her first movie today.”

“You did?” Sophia says with a smile. “What did you see?”

Lydia looks like she wants to answer, but then leans in and buries her face in Clark’s shoulder.

“We saw Peter Pan,” Clark answers, conveying a look that lets Sophia know that Lydia is pretty shy.

“Oh Lydia. I love that movie. Did you like it?”

Lydia turns her head just slightly, looking with just one eye, nodding and smiling.

“So. What do you do here?” Clark asks.

“I work at the hospital. I’m a nurse.”

“Really. It looks like I might be seeing you around then.”

“Why? Do you have a nasty rash or something?” Sophia says playfully.

“No,” Clark says with a hearty chuckle, enjoying the normalcy of life here in the Ark. “I guess I will be working there soon.”

“No kidding. Doing what?

“That’s a good question. But I will pitch in however and wherever I can. I’ll clean toilets if that’s what is needed. It was pretty rough out there. We are just happy to be here, right kiddo?”

Lydia looks up and smiles at Clark, still unable to believe how much their life has changed in such a short amount of time.

“Well, we are so happy to have you here. Both of you.”

The three sit in silence as the pinks and oranges turn to purple and then black as stars begin to emerge. Clark hasn’t felt this happy in a very long time.

CHAPTER TWENTY-FOUR

The next morning, after dropping Lydia off at the park and staying long enough to be convinced that she was going to be okay, Clark was finally able to pry himself away. When he left, Lydia was laughing and smiling as two other girls were showing her how to pump a swing to make it go. Within minutes, she was soaring high into the air, smiling as she watched her shadow move along the ground. As Clark watches her, he is overcome by that strange feeling of déjà vu that has been quite common in the past few days. It's a strange sensation that he hasn't felt in a very long time, but already, he's become accustomed to it, chalking it up to the dramatic change in his life.

Conrad, as he promised, meets Clark at the end of town where the two enjoy lattes and makes some small talk in a bustling coffee shop that is accented with dark, wooden floors and caramel-colored walls. The establishment is staffed with six baristas, which is probably double as many as are needed. Clark finds himself gawking at the people, many of whom wave hello to Conrad as they enter and exit. Just watching people enjoy life, seemingly oblivious to the horrors of this world, makes him both happy and jealous. He wonders to himself if he will ever be able to fully enjoy life after all he has seen.

After about 20 minutes of idle chit chat that mostly consists of Conrad bragging about the facility that he runs, Conrad leads Clark through a set of double doors at the end of town that require a hand scan to access. He then walks past a set of concrete stairs, opting to use the elevator to go just one floor to reach a lower level of the facility. Mostly utilitarian in their appearance, they walk through a gray, concrete corridor with some large, metal tubes, dripping with condensation. After going around the first corner, they arrive at the first stop on the tour. Another hand scan is necessary, clicking a heavy, steel security door, opening into a giant room, hot and humid, five stories high and filled with vegetation. Grow lights permeate the space and a mist systematically comes on and off, watering the entire facility as workers move around the space using metal stairs with platforms every 10 feet, tending to the "fields."

"It is here where we grow tomatoes, potatoes, green beans, carrots, lettuce, peas and much more," Conrad says. "This is one of three hydroponics bays that grow all of the fruits and vegetables that we consume here in the Ark."

"It's truly wondrous. I've never seen anything like it."

"Everything you see here is unique and took decades of trial and error to achieve."

Conrad points to the men and women scattered amongst the space, all doing work of one kind or another.

"We have a full agriculture team, the best and brightest in their fields. They call themselves farmers, but in reality, what they are doing here is beyond anything that has ever been done before. Using cutting-edge technology, they can grow everything twice as fast as usual. With limited soil at their disposal, the team has been able to come up with ways to nourish the ground by using compost after harvest, while infusing it with fertilizers that not only make better, faster growing crops, but keep the soil from losing nutrients."
"It's amazing," Clark says as he walks over to the wall, running his hand across some soft, moist, green vegetation."

"Believe it or not, that one vine actually produces both tomatoes and cucumbers."

"How is that possible?"

"I'd be lying if I told you that I understood it. Apparently, early on, certain plants were a struggle to grow underground. What I know is that many of the plants here are hybrids that co-exist and grow better than either plant could on its own."

"I've never even heard of this type of work."

"That's because it's never been done before. It's like they say, necessity is the mother of invention. I thought that being a man of science, that you might like this."

Conrad likes to walk slow, with his hands clasped behind his back, like a college professor. With a nod of his head, Conrad motions for Clark to follow him as they exit the space.

The two continue on the tour, their next stop being a modest-sized pond with steep concrete walls coming up both sides, much like the old quarry he used to swim in as a kid.

"This does not look very big, but it is actually 50 feet deep and is stocked with tilapia."

"Tilapia?"

"Of course. We need a good source of protein in our diet and tilapia provides that. Not only do they grow to maturity in a short amount of time, but they also eat a special algae that has been specifically put into this tank and is self-sustaining. In short, we do nothing but keep the water oxygenated and at the right temperature, keep the lights on to mimic the sun, and then harvest them as needed."

"Amazing. And this provides enough for the entire town? "Actually there are three similar ponds here too."

"All tilapia?"

"Yes. We tried some others well before the world went dark, but they all proved too difficult to maintain. Tilapia mature quickly, require little in the way of food, and can exist in overcrowded tanks where other species will die.

However, our chef's here have become experts at preparing it in so many varieties, that you would never know it is the same fish."

"So, this is quite possibly the only type of fish left in the world?"

"Well. Not exactly," Conrad says with a wry smile.

"I have a feeling that you are about to blow my mind, again."

Conrad leads Clark through another corridor. After doing a hand and retinal scan, Conrad opens the last of a set of three, large metal doors. Already the temperature has dropped significantly, but when they enter the final room, it is bone chilling. Conrad rubs his arms and makes a show of blowing out his breath in a long, billowy burst. He then points to a series of containers on both sides of a long, skinny room.

"Here is the future, Clark."

Clark looks at him without comprehending, which is exactly what Conrad wanted as he once again puts his hands behind his back and strolls knowingly through the space before continuing. While Clark finds Conrad to be nice, he is also a bit pompous, giving him an arrogant quality. He's the type of guy who loves to hear himself speak and revels in long, dramatic pauses. On the outside before the world went to hell, Clark knew people like Conrad and would probably have disliked him. But considering that only days ago he was toiling above in a world where he would have surely perished sooner than later, Clark has no problem checking his own ego at the door.

"When all is said and done outside, there will be nothing left of the world we once knew. Plant life will likely, slowly, make a comeback. At least some of it will. However, by then, any animal that is not a carnivore will have been long gone. I don't need to tell you that the only animals remaining up top are eating each other.

Clark feels flush even in the frozen space as he knows exactly what Conrad means. Clark hadn't so much as seen an animal in years. He has witnessed firsthand that many of the few remaining people up top have resorted to cannibalism to survive. The atrocities that he and Lydia have seen give them both nightmares almost every night, and probably always will.

"And in just a few more years, most, if not all of them, will also be gone. When the skies clear and levels become acceptable to support human life again, then what?" Conrad asks in the quizzical manner that a tenured college professor would address a class of undergraduates.

Clark shrugs his shoulders, playing the role of the student that he knows he is expected to portray, awaiting the answer from Conrad.

"Noah took each animal onto the Ark in twos for procreation. We think that might take too long, so we took a few more."

Clark walks over to one of the containers, which is frost lined. Conrad smiles, recognizing that Clark now understands. Conrad then grabs one of the handles and opens the hatch, which releases a furious stream of frozen air. He then reaches in and removes one of several canisters. After wiping away some of the frost, Clark sees what appear to be embryos.

"What is it?"

Conrad reads a code on the top and then smiles.

"These are pigs," Conrad says with a smile. In fact, this particular hatch is full of pig embryos, more than 1,000."

"But surely they can't be reanimated."

"Ah. You think not?"

"But this technology. It was in its infancy when …"

"In its infancy as far as the mainstream world was concerned, but in reality, this sort of thing has not only been possible but has been done for decades."

"So, you're saying?"

"That when we re-emerge, we will also re-populate the world, slowly at first, with some of the animals that once lived around the world."

"Just some?"

"Yes. Animals that serve a purpose. Animals that are vital to sustaining life for humans. We saw no need to save say, a Wolverine, Grizzly Bear, or Bengal Tiger. After all, they serve no purpose for humans."

"No purpose?"

"The same goes for Eagles or Hawks. They really do nothing to help the human race, so when we rebuild the world, it will be … in our image I suppose. Earth 2.0 if you will. In simple terms, we will improve upon it.

"You are picking and choosing the species that will survive?"

"Exactly. Now cows, pigs, chickens, deer, turkeys, goats, sheep, and a variety of other important creatures, not to mention countless varieties of fish eggs that have been saved."

"And you are certain that you will be able to grow these creatures? Make them live again?"

"We already have."

Conrad smiles proudly as he rubs his arms, indicating that the cold is now penetrating him and therefore it is time to leave. He carefully puts the tiny pig embryos back in storage, secures the hatch and then leads a perplexed and slightly troubled Clark out of the space.

CHAPTER TWENTY-FIVE

Back in his apartment, Mason sits on the floor, his legs crossed, and hands balanced on his knees. He is deep in meditation, concentrating on his breathing, trying to let his mind go quiet. His accommodations are stark with nothing to personalize the space. To him, it's nothing more than a tool, no different than other necessities such as his gun or knife. He chooses to have no photos, art or knickknacks in his living quarters. To him, those things are completely unnecessary. He has discovered that he is a minimalist, and he doesn't like to have clutter or useless items in his possession.

He needs to shutout distractions so he can think. Trusting his instincts has long been one of his most valued tools. Even as a child, he had a sixth sense about such things, an ability to sense when there is something off about a situation. And right now, his instincts are telling him something isn't right. It's just a feeling, but his feelings have a tendency to be a precursor to something else. For some time now, he has had an uneasy feeling that he can't quite quantify. While he isn't able to explain it, his senses tell him that whatever it is, it is sinister.

His eyes are shut and he is wearing only a pair of white shorts. His body is a roadmap of scars from battles too numerous for him to recall. It's as if they have all begun to blur into one another, each single conflict becoming an ever-shrieking chapter in one large battle. Sometimes at night, he can still see the faces of his victims and recall watching as the life goes out of their eyes. Even he doesn't like to think about the sheer number of people who have breathed their last because of him.

For years he was unable to meditate in such a fashion as the audio implants in his ears pick up every drop of water, the subtle hum of the air filters that constantly clean this subterranean atmosphere, or even his neighbors rolling over in their beds. It was maddening for a while as he felt as though he would never have any peace. He used to beg Ben to remove them, citing that he was going to go mad. In fact, Ben is the one who actually taught Mason how to meditate. Through sheer willpower, he managed to finally overcome this obstacle and by incorporating it into who he is, has made peace with it. Now, when he is in the outside world, it is that superhuman hearing that actually allows him to sleep. He has conditioned himself to hear the sounds of the world like an alarm. Certain sounds do little to rouse him, such as wind or rain, but other noises, such as footfalls or the clanking of weapons, he hears those well before they get close and therefore, is never surprised.

The enhancements to his vision were much easier to get used to. Basically, he went from having 20/25 vision to having something closer to 20/6 vision, which is theorized to be about the visual capability of a young hawk. And the low-light filtering system that was implanted behind his retinas allow him to see better in the dark than any ordinary person.

Those improvements weren't made until Mason was nearly a man, in his teens. However, the physical training, which began much earlier, still haunt him to this day. Long stretches of food and water deprivation, weeks of solitary confinement, endless hours of combat training, pain tolerance sessions that slowly retrained his brain to no longer register pain, these are just some of the things that have turned Mason into the weapon he is now. In fact, after a battle, he has to carefully check himself for wounds or injuries by doing a visual survey since the pain receptors in his brain have been essentially shut off. A couple of years ago, hours after killing six savages armed with homemade shanks, he was having trouble getting comfortable when he laid down. He discovered a broken piece of glass that was four inches long, lodged into his shoulder. It took some effort to reach it and finally dig it out. His body is the same to extreme temperatures as well. To him, 40 degrees and 70 degrees feel almost the same.

He also spent much of his youth with fevers and violent vomiting as part of his training. And it was on those days when he was the sickest that they forced him to train the hardest. There were days when he felt like he was going to die yet was pushed to train for 16 to 20 hours, while being deprived of water and food. There were times where he can barely even remember the training as he was delirious with fatigue. The result of this inhumane treatment is that Mason has not been ill in close to a decade. His body was introduced to sickness regularly, making his adolescence a living hell, creating an immune system unlike any other. He also can push through things that would incapacitate any normal person.

Mason has kept his concerns to himself, unwilling to share with even the few people he is close to. He knows that he cannot, because all he has is a feeling, not proof. So, he continues to follow orders, for the most part.

He is a soldier who has been born and bred for a singular purpose and if he is going to continue to be a valued member of this sanctuary, then he must embrace who he is. He plays his role, that of an efficient soldier who mostly follows orders on the outside and then acts care-free during his stints back in the Ark. But in reality, nothing could be further from the truth. He knows that things here are not as idyllic as they seem.

AUDIO 5

From my youngest days, I was groomed for my role here. Much like you, I never really had a choice, I just didn't realize it. My earliest memories were that of being a patriot for my people. I never questioned it because my father, the most brilliant man I ever knew, made it all seem to make sense. My calling was the most noble it could be. At least that's how it was engrained in me.

Without question, I studied, outworked and outperformed all others and my hard work was rewarded, and I was chosen to be part of the cause. My father was so proud, and I believe my mother also would have relished in my accomplishments if she had lived past my infanthood. My memories of her are of a woman who dedicated her life to being the best mom and wife she could. All these years later, I still miss her daily.

After my mom passed, I spent every hour dedicated to learning. Like a sponge, I threw myself into my studies, likely as a way to shield myself from the sorrow of losing my precious mother. My work paid off as I advanced through high school, college, then medical school with accolades that I have long forgotten about.

My skills as a physician and scientist were rewarded as I lived like a king before the virus hit. Only the purest bloodline would be chosen. Perfection was the goal. I was then asked to take perfection and improve upon it.

Look around the Ark. Look at its inhabitants. Notice anything unusual? How could you? You and everybody else that were handpicked don't know any different. Genetic perfection, nothing else. A club foot or cleft pallet would have been unacceptable. Every person here was picked for, screened, and ultimately chosen for their perfection. You think you were accidentally discovered? You, like everybody else here, was on a list.

Over the years, I have cared for you, the residents, the administrators, and the rest of the Legion, but you have always been special to me. There's not a day that goes by when I haven't regretted my role in your life. I was following orders, but now I see that my belief in the cause was nothing more than deception that I was too foolish to see.

You could have had a real life. You are smart and caring, but early testing showed that you had superior physical prowess and for that reason and that reason alone, you were transformed into a warrior. The physical and mental training you endured is nothing that I would wish on anybody. But it's my role that I am truly sorry for. The years where you were so sick that you nearly died as I introduced your body to ever-increasing doses of illness, poisons and bacteria to build your immune system into what it now is. Those years of suffering have made you immune to things that would kill anybody else.

I also regret and want to apologize to you for all of the surgical procedures as the goal was to improve upon the physical condition. The results did work as you are superior to any other human being, including the rest of your team. Your strength allowed us to go further than we could with the others who would not have survived. In essence, your strength has also been your curse and is the reason for all the suffering you endured in your youth.

While your training was closely monitored, I included a few secrets that nobody else knows about, one of which you are now hearing. I trust almost nobody, but I trust you. Now, I hope you will trust me.

CHAPTER TWENTY-SIX

Rachel is in the lab at the hospital, looking through the results of a blood test. Her blonde hair is pulled back into a ponytail, highlighting her high cheekbones and large, blue eyes. Her lab coat hangs off her as her thin frame seemingly gets absorbed into the large, unflattering garment. Her face is sullen, concern welling up in her as she finishes the procedure, one that she already knows the outcome.

Rachel was a gifted student but when the skies went dark, she was still quite young. Therefore, the majority of her medical training comes from working in the Ark. While she proved to be a quick study and learned quite well, it was because of Ben and her father, Fredrich, who were friends, that she had the opportunities to work in the medical field. If it hadn't been for that, she could have just as easily been given the designation as an unskilled worker in town. Either way, her ticket to the Ark was punched long ago due equally to her clean bloodline as well as her father's heavy financial investment to the facility.

But she has more than proven herself and is now a highly valued and trusted member of the Ark. One who is well aware of the agenda of this place, something not everybody is privy to. She knows what the goal is and whether she agrees with it or not is irrelevant. Nothing she does or doesn't do could change that. That is until now.

Rachel is re-examining the blood she has taken from Lydia and Clark. She knows she should not be doing this. Protocol dictates that she reports any and all abnormal results immediately. But she finds herself praying that the first sample was somehow incorrect.

After taking some time to look through the whirling machine, watching through a small porthole as the centrifuge divides Lydia's genetic material again, Rachel is hoping that she is wrong, which is why she is retesting. But deep down, she knows she has made no error.

Clark's DNA, as expected, came back within the acceptable parameters. After all, his lineage had already been researched before Mason brought him here. Lydia on the other hand is most obviously not pure in blood. Rachel could tell that as soon as she saw her but was still hoping for a miracle. But Lydia's blood contains the genomes that she feared when she first laid eyes on her. This is unenviable news to be sure. For a fleeting moment, she thinks about trying to hide the results. After all, she poses no imminent risk. Besides, she is so young. Almost immediately she shudders, thinking about how there are no secrets in the Ark. Ben told her as much. She doesn't even want to think about what that could mean if she attempted to withhold this information.

But what will this mean for Lydia? At the very least, she will be sterilized. The administrators cannot and will not ever risk the pollution of a pure blood line. Her test shows direct roots to the Middle East and those results certainly show some traits of Jewish ancestry. No other races will be tolerated, but that one is particularly loathed by the council. She's a little girl who did nothing wrong. A child brought into a barren, violent world. The fact that she lived as long as she did on the outside is a miracle in itself.

Most who live in the Ark are either too young, oblivious or choose not to think about the reason they have been chosen to live. Only a few, like herself, are fully aware of the reason that diversity does not exist in the Ark. But now she has been made aware of the fact that there is another hidden agenda. Only days before he died, Ben told her "Be careful Rachel, things are not as they seem here."

A brilliant physician, he was an amazing mentor who taught her so much. While he and the others are sworn to protect the pure bloodline, it was other factors that began to trouble him. Things that didn't seem to serve the ultimate purpose of the Ark. He had been pre-occupied, doing a lot of extra research in the lab. It even became an obsession with him at one point as he was spending nearly every waking hour doing research and experiments. She chalked it up to being an eccentric genius. But what did he mean by his warning to her?

After his death, each council member individually tried to console her, telling her that the doctor had been a valued member of the Ark and his contribution will be remembered in the re-writing of history when the inhabitants finally emerge and take back the earth.

She didn't believe them then and she certainly doesn't trust them now. But what choice does she have?

CHAPTER TWENTY-SEVEN

Lydia sits on a fake lawn that looks and feels almost like the real thing, not that she or any of the other children there know what real grass is supposed to feel like. It's similar to the material that was once used in football stadiums where 75,000 people would gather to spend obscene amounts of money to cheer on their favorite team. Now, all that is left of the technology that created this artificial grass is deep underground in this park.

Lydia is dressed in a white sundress, the first dress she has ever owned. She and Clark were taken on a shopping spree a few days after they arrived, picking out numerous outfits. The people who worked at the clothing shops were so helpful. Lydia couldn't believe how much interest the workers took in helping her pick out just the right clothing. At first, she felt very self-conscious in the dress, but after meeting some of the other girls in the Ark and seeing that they dress similar to her, she adapted quickly to her new look. In fact, things like bathing, brushing her hair and checking out her appearance in the mirror were such foreign concepts to her that Clark had to sit her down and teach her the importance of it. On the outside, nobody cared how they looked, so it is going to take some time for her to get used to this new facet of life.

Lydia is flanked on both sides by blonde-haired little girls as they play a board game called "Candyland." The rules are quite simple and even though her only education on the outside was some rudimentary mathematics and basic grammar, she picked up the game quite quickly. Not very long ago, she had never even seen candy, but now, thanks to the Sweet Shoppe in town, she has learned the wonders of lollipops, cookies and her new favorite discovery, chocolate.

Tia and Becca are the names of the 8-year-old girls who look like they could be twins, but actually are not related.

After finishing one of the games, Tia lets out a little squeal of excitement, raising her arms in victory. Becca rolls her eyes, sticks out her tongue and then falls over onto her back, giggling. After a moment, Lydia copies the behavior, trying to learn how to be a little girl.

"Let's play again," Tia says.

"Forget it. You've won three in a row," Becca says with a playful frown.

"Come on. Please."

"Let's play something else," Becca says.

"Okay. But what?"

"Jacks?"

"No."

"Uno?"

"Lame," Tia says.

"Tag?"

"No."

They sit quietly for a moment, trying to figure out what to do next, and then Tia's eyes light up.

"Truth or dare?" Tia finally says, talking about a game she heard about from one of the older kids.

"Okay." Becca says.

"Don't-Know-How," Lydia says, her voice still shaky, only starting to begin to utter a few phrases in her short time since entering the Ark.

"Oh. It's easy," says Tia. "All you have to do is say either truth or dare. If you pick truth, you have to answer a question honestly. If you pick dare, then you have to try to do something that one of the other players says. I'll go first so you can see how to play."

"Okay Tia. Truth or dare?" Becca says.

"Uh. Truth. I guess"

"Okay. Let's see … What should I ask you? Oh, I have it. Do you think that Brian from our class is cute?"

Tia starts giggling all crazy and Becca joins in. Lydia smiles, not knowing what to say, but intrigued by the game.

"Forget it. I'm not answering that," Tia shouts.

"You have to Tia. It's the rule."

"I don't want to answer that question. It's silly."

"You have to," Becca says, giggling hard.

"No. He's not," Tia finally says with a big smile.

"Tia. You have to tell the truth."

After a long pause, she finally nods her head.

"Yes. He's really, really cute." Tia admits.

All three girls start laughing and pointing at each other. Lydia has never even thought about whether or not somebody is cute. In fact, she has only seen a handful of children in her entire life prior to coming to the Ark.

"Okay. I'm next," says Becca.

"Truth or dare," Tia says, looking at Lydia and winking.

"Uh. Truth," Becca says. "No, wait. I mean dare. I pick dare."

"Do a back handspring," Tia says.

"That's easy."

Becca kicks off her blue shoes, jumps to her feet, gets a short run and then performs a very good back handspring. Lydia's dark eyes get huge as she claps and cheers for a maneuver that she has never seen before. Lydia has never simply played. Life on the outside didn't lend itself to carefree fun. It was all about survival, nothing else.

"Okay Lydia. It's your turn now. Truth or dare," Tia says as Becca bounds over and plops down beside her, getting a high five for her effort, something she has never seen before. Lydia thinks about it for a moment and knows she could never pull off a move like Becca just did. It takes her more than 20 seconds to choose as the two girls prod her to pick one or the other.

"Truth?" she says with uncertainty in her voice.

Tia looks at her very seriously for a moment and then blurts out, "Have you ever seen a dead body before?"

"Tia!" Becca scolds.

"What? It's just a question. She lived outside her whole life. I hear that there are monsters up there that eat people."

"Are not," Becca says.

"Yes sir. My friend says there are giant lizard people who hunt humans and that's why we stay inside all of the time. Until they are all gone."

"You are so stupid," Becca says.

"You're stupid!" Tia growls, before turning her attention to Lydia. "You never answered the question."

Lydia has seen tons of dead bodies and has seen many people killed, including the young men that tried to attack her and Mason killed. She has begun to tremble. A minute ago, she was having so much fun. But now all she wants to do is run away. This game took a very nasty turn and Lydia is not sure how to respond.

"Well? We are waiting," Tia demands, crossing her arms.

"Leave her alone. You're not being nice," Becca scolds.

Lydia's eyes are big and spooked. She doesn't even like to think about how many dead bodies she has seen. She most certainly doesn't want to talk about it.

"Lydia," she hears the friendly voice that rescues her. She quickly jumps to her feet and runs over to Clark who is just emerging in the park and heard nothing of the conversation. "Hi sweetie. Having fun?"

Lydia doesn't answer, but instead hugs him around the waist, squeezing him as tight as she can.

"Whoa. Hey. I wasn't gone that long. So, you hungry? It's just about lunch time I hear."

She nods in agreement, happy for any excuse to leave the park and those girls.

"Tell your friends' good-bye," he tells her and she offers a wave to them, eager to get away from that conversation.

As soon as they are out of earshot, Tia turns to Becca.

"Did you see what color her eyes are? They're like black."

"I think they're brown."

"It's freaky. And her hair is so dark. It looks like it is full of dirt. I've never seen hair that color."

"I don't think it's dirty. I think that's just how she is," Becca says.

"I think she got infected with something when she lived up there and it turned her eyes and hair dark."

"You think so?"

"Yeah. You touched her. That's probably going to happen to you now. I bet your eyes are going to turn black, too."

"Shut up," Becca says, tears in her eyes.

"You're going to be a freak just like her and they are going to kick you out and make you live up top with the lizards."

Becca gets up, crying and runs off, while a satisfied Tia sits and begins putting away the board game.

CHAPTER TWENTY-EIGHT

Guiding the exhausted women, Colin pulls them along by a rope that is tied around each one's neck. The flesh around their throats is raw from rope burns as anytime they slow down too much for his liking, Colin gives it a hard tug. The young, black women are shivering, half naked, nearly skin and bones. Neither looks to be older than about 14. Conrad will be pleased.

Barefoot and exhausted, the young women have glazed over eyes. For most of their lives, they have been survivors, avoiding others, staying hidden, continuing to live while most perish. But now, both find themselves yearning for death, something that will elude them.

Colin, the Legion member who is Conrad's favorite errand boy, could have gone around a trampled down thicket of long dead but still painful field of thorns, but he gets a sickening thrill from seeing the agony of the razor-sharp needles stabbing the women in the feet and legs. He has always enjoyed seeing others in pain and this is no different.

The wind is cutting through the young women, as Colin has removed most of their layers, leaving them with just a couple thin rags. They are both shivering so hard that it is making it hard for them to walk.

After a long, winding hike, Colin drags the suffering teens down into a canyon to a long-since dried up creek bed. They continue along the rocky terrain, following the path of the old tributary until they reach a bend in the path where both sides are guarded by high, rock walls. It is there where the sentinels can see in all directions from hidden cameras that line the region. Security is of the utmost importance near any of the entry points and nobody will be let in until the technicians that man the security cameras are 100-percent certain that Colin has not been followed.

While this portion of the landscape looks like any other, it is actually all manmade, to look like nothing out of the ordinary, but allows for 360-degree views for miles in all directions.

The women, realizing they are stopping, both collapse to the ground, their ebony limbs intertwined, exhausted. Colin will wait here as long as necessary, standing at attention, senses sharp for anything out of the ordinary.

After a 45-minute wait, a metal clicking can be heard and the hollow scraping of rock becomes audible. Colin jerks hard on the rope, rousing both women who had passed out. Not wanting to endure more punishment from this sadistic man, they obediently stand on shaky legs. Their dark, frightened eyes watch in confusion as a large rock rises off the ground, guided by four, steel beams, lifting to five feet into the air, revealing a flat, concrete slab with a steel-lined hole carved into the Earth. They are dragged over to the entrance where Colin shoves them both to the ground. They then are ordered to take turns climbing down a ladder into total darkness. Both women are so exhausted and weak that they can barely make it. When both of the terrified women enter the space, Colin follows, the hole closing up before he is even to the bottom of the 25-foot ladder. When the hatch is secured, a harsh light comes on, causing both women to squint and cover their eyes.

Colin grabs the rope again, giving one of the women a hard, back-handed slap in the face for stumbling into him, and then pulls them down the orange, brick corridor to a big, metal hatch. Colin waits until security eventually pops the latch and he opens it, dragging both women through before shutting and sealing the door. Colin then pulls them down a white, round hallway. At the end, he stops in front of a large mirror, moves back to the young women and aggressively strips each of them of their remaining clothes, tearing the rags off and dropping them to the floor. The women, who are indeed teenage sisters, stand there trembling. Even through the filth and malnutrition, their thin frames and long legs arouse something primal in Conrad as he looks on from behind the one-way glass.

Conrad licks his lips like a hungry predator. These might be the best so far. Colin has again delivered, completed his mission. But it will take some time before Conrad can taste these forbidden fruits. A few weeks of food, some time to heal those wounds, not to mention multiple cleansings, and these two will do quite nicely. Quite nicely indeed.

Both will be shown der Kerker first, and it will be explained to them that they will comply completely with any and all orders. The first time they disobey, that hellhole will be their new homes. After seeing the horror of that place, Conrad is quite certain that they will fall in line and be obedient sex slaves as the others have.

CHAPTER TWENTY-NINE

Before the bulging muscles, prior to the surgical enhancements, a scrawny, blonde-haired boy is struggling with every fiber of his being, pushing his body to its very limit. A 10-year-old Mason claws his way up a rocky, mountain trail, ahead of the other candidates that are struggling behind. Many of the boys keep stopping to vomit or simply fall as their legs give out. But not Mason. While he also feels the effects of the toxin they are being given that cause severe nausea, chills and fatigue, he wills himself forward, continuing up the trail, his body shivering as fever has enveloped him. While he feels as though he is operating in a haze, he is able to concentrate on the task before him. He is beginning to be able to ignore the suffering his body is going through and still function. It is something that few are able to do.

At the top of a steep grade, he has enough of his wits remaining to roll to the left to avoid a barrage of heavy bean bags fired from a handheld weapon that is known as a stun gun. If hit in the body, the force is enough to incapacitate, if hit in the head, it will render him unconscious. He clamors along the edge of a ridge that he uses for cover, the projectiles hissing through the air, narrowly missing his head. Mason hugs the ridge, scrambling through some thick vegetation, until he gets out of the open.

He can hear the instructors moving to intercept him, so he cuts through a heavily wooded area full of thorn bushes, knowing they will not follow. Using the element of surprise, he reemerges minutes later, past where he anticipated an ambush site, reacquiring the trail, bounding fallen logs armed with razor wire. After half running, half falling down a muddy valley, he nears the end of the course as he enters the flat where he is greeted by three, full-grown men in tactical gear. Without pausing, he sprints to the right, evading the first man and then, executing a diving roll, grabs a handful of mud before springing to his feet and hitting the second soldier in the face with it, blinding him temporarily.

The third man takes a hard slash with his baton but misses badly as Mason anticipated the move and ducked the blow while executing a nasty sidekick to the top of the ankle, breaking the bone and sending the man sprawling to the ground with a scream. Hearing the first man's boots clumsily stomping behind him, Mason drops to a knee, spins and lands a perfectly executed palm strike, with an upward thrust to the man's testicles, dropping him to the ground like a stone. Mason then sprints the final 20 yards to the buzzer, the pursuers all unable to stop him. He is poised to be the first to ever complete the course. With the finish line within his grasp, electricity fills his body only a few feet away from the elusive ending to the course, dropping him to the ground in a heap, where his body spasms and convulses for several seconds.

After finishing the brutal course more than eight minutes ahead of the closest competitor, his reward was to be tazed just seconds away from completing the course. Of course, that was all part of the plan. If anybody was able to complete the entire course, which has never happened, a hidden soldier was instructed to drop the young candidate with enough juice to completely incapacitate him. After all, failure is absolutely part of the training, and this young man cannot be permitted to succeed.

The trainer walked over to Mason, a pompous scoff on his face as he looked down at the twitching boy. What was all the more surprising was when Mason, who was using a technique Ben explained to him called "playing possum," spun on his hip, hitting the soldier in the face with a rock before yanking the wires from his body and then leaping to his feet, diving across the line and hitting the buzzer that chimes loudly. He stands there victoriously, a scowl stretched across his dirty face, fearless as usual. The buzzer continues to chime and he stands defiantly.

From that day on, the instructors were exponentially harder on Mason than any of the other candidates, yet he also earned their respect as none ever underestimated him again.

That was just one in a myriad of days during his youth where Mason not only passed his training session, but actually exceeded all expectations. Often when Mason has drifted off to sleep, his subconscious will recall moments from his past, both good and bad. What he remembers even more about that day is the smell of the vegetation, the warmth of the sun, being out in the real world. That was before the world fell and the underground existence began.

Mason is jarred from his slumber when all the lights go off with a loud, snapping sound, causing him to jerk wide awake, immediately ready for combat. He then quickly realizes there is no danger, he was dreaming, and his session is simply over. He pushes the lid off this glorified coffin, climbs out of it and grabs a towel and wipes the perspiration off his body before putting on his briefs.

Everybody who lives in the Ark must take part in sessions under the lights, which have been specially designed to mimic the positive effects that the sun used to give to people before the clouds covered the Earth. Mason is told that years ago, similar devices were used by people who wanted to get a tan. Now, a slight glow to the skin is simply the side effect of the lights, which not only help with Vitamin D production in the body, but are also beneficial in staving off psoriasis, eczema, depression and even help promote healthy growth in children.

Additionally, every light in the Ark has been fitted with similar lights, only at a much lower level, to create the feeling of well-being that the sun can provide.

Mason emerges from the small room, his skin a rosy red. After nearly two months on the outside, his body will take a few sessions to get used to the treatments again. Standing in just a pair of briefs, his impressive physique catches the eye of the young technician, who smiles, embarrassed that she got busted gazing at Mason, who is somewhat of a celebrity in the Ark. Mason smiles a bit, walking toward her and stopping so she can finish the treatment. Trying to remain professional, she examines Mason with a special light and a small, digital camera, marking her findings on a chart. Part of her job is to catalog any new changes in the skin. For most, they are just screening for any potential skin cancer from the treatments. For Mason, she also has a couple new scars to add to his file.

"Okay Mason," says the blonde-haired, blue-eyed girl of 25 years old as she taps a keyboard. "You are all done. Next appointment is on Saturday, July 17, at 2 p.m. Does that work for you?

"Michelle, do you ever wonder why we keep the date?"

"Sorry. What?

"Just wondering. Doesn't it seem kind of absurd to keep track of the date in here?"

"Uh. Well. I never really thought about it. I guess we need it though. You know, for keeping appointments, for instance."

"I guess so. Just seems strange to me is all."

"What do you suggest?"

"I don't know. How about just days. For instance, the first day here would have been Number 1. Five years would have been day 1,826. You know what I mean?"

Mason continues to dress, putting on khaki-colored pants and a light-green T-shirt.

"Seems kind of impersonal," she says. "Saying Wednesday sounds much more friendly than, say, Day 724."

"It just seems weird to me to keep using June, July, etc."

"How else would we know if it was Christmas?"

"Ah. Good point. Holidays." Mason says with sarcasm.

"Easter. Valentine's Day."

"Arbor Day," he adds.

"Huh?" she says with a giggle.

"Groundhog Day. Flag Day. Margarita Day."

"What?"

"Never mind. Just thinking out loud I guess."

"Maybe you think too much," she offers, handing him a small bottle of lotion.

"Well, that's something I'm not usually accused of."

"Put that lotion on twice a day. It will help keep your skin from getting flaky."

"What if I can't reach everywhere?" he says with a smile. "Should I call you?"

She smiles and goes over to a computer console and punches in some numbers, giggling nervously, the young technician who has had a crush on Mason since she began this job. She doesn't know what to say, so she changes the subject.

"According to your chart, you are going to need extra sessions following so much time outside."

"So, we get to spend even more time together? How can I say no?" he says.

After a moment on the keyboard, she looks up at Mason with a serious look on her face.

"What do you do out there? What's it like?"

"You know I'm not permitted to discuss that. It's classified."

"I know, but can't you tell me anything?"

"Well, I guess I can trust you with one thing."

"What? What is it?" she eagerly says.

"Promise you won't tell on me?"

"Of course."

"I don't know. If anybody finds out I talked about …"

"I promise. I won't say anything," she says with desperation, starved to know exactly what is going on out there.

Mason looks around suspiciously, as if he thinks somebody might be listening. Then, cupping his hands and whispering he says, "Starbucks is still open."

"What?"

"Starbucks. They are everywhere up there."

"Sorry I asked."

"Even during the apocalypse, people need their coffee."

"Whatever," she says with a frown of her pouty lips.

"What? You wanted to know something."

"See you next week."

"I'm serious."

Realizing that Mason isn't going to tell her anything about the outside, she looks back at her computer screen.

"Okay. So next week then, Saturday, July 17, 2 p.m., does that work?"

"No way. That's World Juggler's Day," he exclaims.

"Is not," she says with a flirty giggle and a flip of her bouncy, curly blonde hair.

"It most definitely is. But, if that's all you have available, then fine, I'll move a few things around," he says, having looked up a list of holidays for the following week before arriving, knowing she will search it after he leaves to see if he's right.

"Okay. I'm booking your for then."

"I look forward to it," he says with a wink.

Mason smiles and calmly leaves the small room where a waiting area has five others waiting for their appointments. Mason exits the medical facility and begins walking down the street, waving to those who wave to him, but lost in thought as he looks at all the faces in the town, hard at work, void of any true diversity. He's been on the outside long enough to know that the inhabitants of the Ark are not a very true representation of the occupants on the outside. Clearly this is by design. But why?

While the Ark is a utopic existence compared to what is going on outside, it's not perfect and there are many secrets he has uncovered over the years. Mason has never spoken to anybody else about his findings or theories as he doesn't know who he can trust, if anybody.

What he does know for sure is that some of the other Legion members also go outside from time-to-time and he is certain that their orders are not the same as his.

CHAPTER THIRTY

Vance Cole has been in the Ark since the beginning. He was brought here for his prowess as a scientist. His parents were so proud of him. Unfortunately, they were not permitted to come. After all, while they were both intelligent people who were also minor financiers for the cause, they were too old and didn't have the skill set necessary for the limited occupancy. He hates the thought of what their lives must've been like, but they were such believers in this cause and told their son that the best way to honor them would be to do his job well. And that's exactly what he did.

He knows he was lucky to be spared the horrors of the outside world. Small in stature and slightly built, he always excelled in academics rather than athletics. On the outside, he knows he wouldn't have fared too well. His parents sacrificed everything so he could have this chance, which is why he makes sure to work very hard each and every day. For many years, he never questioned anything he did. But over time, he began to see things that didn't add up. It was small things at first, but then, over the years, he began being exposed to more and more. In the past few months, he has gleaned that much of what he is being asked to do is amoral.

But when Ben Carlson died, it confirmed much of what Vance had also begun to suspect. That their work was not being perfected to be used for good as had been promised. It has taken months for him to work up the courage, but Vance finally decided that he must unburden himself to somebody. He can no longer sleep very well; his appetite is being affected as his stomach is upset every day and he doesn't know where to turn.

In the manic way that only an OCD scientist who is now completely paranoid can, Vance asks Rachel to meet him on a catwalk outside the lab that overlooks the underwater river that is the lifeblood of this underground sanctuary. Rachel doesn't have access to this part of the facility, so it took some convincing to get her to meet and follow him through the labyrinth of access tunnels to get to the destination. It is there, with the sounds of rushing water and void of much technology that he feels he can speak in hushed tones without being heard or recorded. At first, Rachel feared that the skinny, blonde scientist had romance on his mind and would have to gently let him down – or possibly toss him into the river, she muses with a smile.

However, the second she sees his face, full of angst, she realizes he has something serious to discuss. While always pale looking, Vance looks downright gaunt and ghostly in appearance, and he wears the bloodshot eyes of a man who is exhausted.

"I assume doctor-patient confidentiality is still a thing," he whispers, his eyes haunted and frightened.

"I hope you're not asking me to give you an exam on this shaky catwalk," she jokes, trying to lighten the mood. "You could get really injured."

"I'm serious, Rachel. I need to know that what I'm about to tell you will remain a secret."

"Vance. Of course. What's wrong?" she says, seeing the angst on his face and detecting the trembling in his voice.

After some trepidation and anxious, deep breaths, Vance finally wills himself past his terror and speaks.

"Rachel. Do you know what kind of work I do?"

"Sure. You're a chemist. It's because of you that we have all the comforts of home," she says with a warm smile, trying to be comforting.

"At first, I worked to help us breathe better air and synthesize cleaner water. But once things began working well, I was pulled from that work and given a new task."

"Task?"

“Yes. I was called into a private session and told there was something really important for me to head up.”

“How flattering,” Rachel offers, not knowing what else to say.

“It was weird though. It was just myself and Tod.”

“Not the rest of the council?”

“No.”

“Still. The fact that you were chosen for something big. That’s great.”

“That’s what I thought … at first. I was taken to a wing below that I never even knew existed.”

“We have a facility below the basement level?”

“Oh yes. It is vast, full of technology that nearly nobody else has ever seen. And I have not seen it all. Even with all the filtration systems and dehumidifiers, it’s below the river line and therefore always has a cold dampness in the air. It was there that I was introduced to a material I had heard about, but never seen before.”

“What was it?”

“The material was never commercialized. But I had learned about it from a European scientist at a symposium many years ago.”

“Okay. So exactly what is it?”

“Years before we entered the Ark, a team of scientists in Denmark were working to synthesize crystalline materials that could bind and store oxygen in high concentrations. In the early years of this science, a couple of ounces of this granular substance was enough to absorb all of the usable oxygen in a space the size of a bathtub.

“During its genesis, the belief was that storing huge reserves of pure oxygen would be vital for long space missions or for domes and other structures built on other worlds. The next step was to reverse the process, so that the stored oxygen could be released. This would allow 100 times, or more, of the O2 to be stored and transported. In fact, the technology was getting close to having practical applications and rumored to be in the works for use on potential Martian outposts before our own world fell into chaos.

"I was told that the focus was to allow our citizens higher and purer oxygen to better the lives of everybody. As you know, our O2 levels here are well within the acceptable range, but not nearly as high as in the outside world before the skies went dark.

"My work has been exclusively focused on improving this material and enhancing it."

"Okay. That's great. But why all the cloak and dagger, Vance? This doesn't sound like something too terrible."

"The science behind it works like this. It is a selective chemisorption process that senses oxygen and essentially absorbs it so rapidly that it is funneled directly into the material and stored. Over the years, I have made some huge enhancements."

"By yourself?"

"Mostly I work alone. A few times I've had to bring in some people to assist. But never sharing the whole process with them. Those are Tod's orders. Often, I would work with just Tod. Believe it or not, he's a brilliant scientist. He's the most intelligent man I've ever met. His concepts and intuition are groundbreaking and with my knowledge of chemistry helped push boundaries that I never thought possible.

"With each round of tests, breaking the material down at the molecular level, we were able to make the material more and more potent. In test facilities on the lower level, the material has been refined to the point that only a few grains will remove all oxygen in a 20-meter-by-20-meter room in 15 seconds."

"My God, Vance. That's amazing."

"It was also during that final round of tests that I discovered something that I never thought possible. Something terrifying."

"What was it?"

"I discovered that what we created didn't have an off switch."

"What do you mean?"

"I mean. The material is so potent that it actually increases."

"You mean it grows? Like a sponge?"

"No. That's the frightening part. It actually began splitting at a rate unlike anything ever thought possible. As it absorbs oxygen, it actually reproduces. A few grains of this material when introduced to oxygen rich air removes all O2, leaving exponentially more grains than the few we started with."

"That's amazing, and kind of scary Vance."

"In one test, I only used 10 grains of the material in an oxygen-rich room. When I went back, there were hundreds of oxygen-saturated grains all over the floor. All that was left was nothing but 99-percent nitrogen, with a dash of argon, xenon, hydrogen, helium, krypton and carbon dioxide making up that that final 1 percent."

"Meaning?"

"Meaning that it takes all the oxygen and leaves pure poison in its place."

"What did you do?"

"The first thing was to continually pump more oxygen into the space, keeping it running for days on end."

"And?"

"Each grain kept splitting, over and over. The more O2, the more storage cells, or grains, it produced. I had hoped that eventually, it would stop. But test after test showed that the reaction in ceaseless. In fact, the only way to stop it was to gather up every, oxygen-saturated grain, and place them in an air-tight container."

"When you discovered this, what did you do?"

"I told Tod that we needed to meet with the council to tell them about our findings. What was supposed to be a way to store oxygen had turned into something quite dangerous. If some of it were accidentally released into the Ark, can you imagine what could happen?

"What did Tod say?"

"He told me that nobody besides he and I could know about our discovery."

"Why?"

"I don't know. But the way he said it to me, it chilled me to the core. His eyes looked dead and black, like a shark, and his words penetrated me down to my bones."

"So, he threatened you?"

"Well, he never said anything threatening, but his meaning came through loud and clear."

"What happened next?"

"I continued to work for the next couple of weeks, doing my job as instructed by Tod. Then one day, I was told I was getting an assistant."

"An assistant?"

"Ben Carlson."

"Ben. Why?"

"Because they needed to see how it affected a living subject. And it was decided that his expertise was necessary. After all, I work in chemistry, but Ben is an actual medical doctor. So, we began experimenting with lab mice. We'd put them in a room, then introduce a few grains of the substance. Then, afterwards Ben would autopsy the mice. Tod was fascinated by the technology."

"I'm still a little lost, Vance."

Vance takes a deep breath, looking around nervously even though the two are clearly alone. Then, he finally proceeds.

"One day, shortly after Ben died, I had a new subject to test it on."

"What kind of subject, Vance?" Rachel asks with a cold shutter starting to climb her spine.

"It. It was. A woman."

"What?" Rachel gasps.

"I didn't want to. But Tod ordered me. Ordered me to do it and swore me to secrecy in the same menacing way that told me if I didn't do exactly as I was told that I would be eliminated."

"A woman? What woman?"

"Nobody I'd ever seen before. She wasn't … wasn't one of us."

"One of us?"

"She was Asian."

"From where? How?"

"I don't know!" Vance hisses, urging Rachel to lower her voice. "And she wasn't the only one."

"More?"

"Countless more. People of various genders, races and ages."

"Oh God, Vance. Why are you telling me this now?"

"Do you remember when Ben died?

"Yes. Had a heart attack and died while working in the lower level. He was in his mid-seventies."

"The night he died, Tod, Ben and myself were there. I had been working for about 14 hours straight, with them joining me later in the day. Tod and Ben had been arguing about something. Their relationship had become strained over a period of days."

"What caused the disagreement."

"I don't know, but the tension was palpable. On that night, Tod said that I should go get some rest. I was happy because not only was I so tired that I could barely keep my eyes open, but the dynamic between them was also terribly uncomfortable. So, I went back to my apartment and went to bed."

"But Ben was found alone, right?"

"Yes. I found him the next day. It was a nightmare. I immediately called Tod, who came down and knelt by his body."

"It was definitely tragic. It was unfortunate. But it was just his time. His heart gave out."

"At first, I though the same thing. But now, I don't think that's how he died."

"What do you mean?"

"I mean the purple face, burst eye vessels and dried blood on his nose. After Ben's death, Tod started bringing in human subjects from what he deemed impure races. He called them animals. Ben looked identical to how the human test subjects looked after being exposed to Reinigen."

"Reinigen?"

"That's the name Tod gave the substance."

"What exactly are you saying, Vance?"

"I think Ben and Tod were arguing about using humans for testing. I believe Ben refused to be part of it. Then, on the night he died, I believe he went in to remove the material and test it for its absorption percentage, something that is standard for us when testing on mice. But the door was somehow shut and sealed behind him."

"Did somebody shut the air off?"

"No. That's the frightening part. The O2 was on full, yet no oxygen was present in the room when Ben was found. But I found saturated Reinigen granules on the floor. The material absorbed any and all oxygen even before it entered the room. Ben suffocated.

"Where was Tod?" Rachel asks.

"Yes. Where was Tod?

Fear grips Rachel as she knows that Ben told her to be careful. That things in the Ark are not what they seem. His findings are likely what cost him his life.

CHAPTER THIRTY-ONE

Friedrich and Johan are Legion members who are in charge of the training for these three teens who have been chosen to attempt to become part of the Legion. While Mason and Gibby are more gifted soldiers, these two have no compassion and are ruthless in their training. For that reason, they are in charge of this portion of training. Most of these boys will not make it. The training is so brutal that most will ultimately wash out. These three boys do not live in the Ark during the training. In fact, none of them have seen anybody other than their trainers for nearly three months. They've all be picked for their physical prowess as well as passing a series of psychological exams.

This lower level of the facility has everything they need for the training. There is a fitness facility with weights, cardio equipment and a variety of heavy bags. There is also a strategic training room where the young men learn how to be effective warriors. For any that move on, weapons training will commence. They sleep on a concrete floor with only a small pillow and blanket. The boys all look gaunt and sickly as they are in the throes of the part of the training where they are given measured doses of a variety of illnesses in an attempt to strengthen their immune systems. It's the same thing that all prospective Legion members must endure.

On this day, the boys, who are half-starved to teach them how to function while weak and ill, are in the battle room, standing at attention, awaiting instruction. They have been standing for nearly 90 minutes, the room's temperature turned up to the mid-90s. Johan is walking around them, holding a baton, awaiting Friedrich to return. The boys are not permitted to move at all, but due to their situation, this is nearly impossible. The smallest boy, named Kenneth, who has a black eye and whose blonde hair is plastered to his head from sweat, strains not to move but his fever causes him to shiver, which turns into a shudder, causing his upper body to sway. Johan sees this and walks up behind him, promptly smashing him across the shoulder blades with the baton, knocking the small, pale boy to the floor. A second boy, named Julian, turns his head to look at Kenneth and he is met with a baton to the back of his legs, dropping him to the ground as well.

"Up!" Johan shouts, forcing both boys to struggle back to their feet.

After several more moments, Friedrich returns holding a tray with two plates of food. There is fish, potatoes, rolls, peas and even a slice of pie on each plate. The sweet smell fills the space and the boys involuntarily salivate as they haven't had much to eat for the past 10 days. Friedrich puts the plates on a table and then addresses the boys who are all wearing beige pants tucked into their black boots and green T-shirts, neatly tucked in.

"There are two plates of food," Friedrich announces. "One plate per person. You have 10 minutes to eat the food and then the plates will be removed. No sharing. Time starts now."

Adding a component of psychological torture is a tool used to ensure that all Legion members learn that weakness will not be tolerated. The three boys look at each other, unsure how to proceed. After half a minute, the largest of the boys, a brown-haired recruit with freckles speckled across his nose and cheeks, walks over toward the table. The other two follow suit and converge on the table.

"One of these plates is mine," the large boy says. "You two can decide who gets the other one."

"Why should you get one, Michael?" Kenneth asks.

"Because I am the biggest and the strongest. That's why."

Clearly this kid has been the bully of the group as he is likely the one who has been winning the sparring sessions. However, the other two have obviously been talking about it because as Michael reaches for the plate, in a flash, they attack him. Kenneth grabs both legs while Julian lands a hard punch to the side of Michael's face, as all three tumble to the ground. The two smaller boys begin unloading punches on Michael, obviously knowing they cannot let up if they are going to eat today. However, it only takes a moment for the tide to turn as Michael grabs Kenneth by the head and thrusts his knee up, catching the boy flush on the jaw, knocking him unconscious. Michael then turns quickly, throws Julian onto the ground, pounces on him, straddling his chest in a combat position known as full mount, and begins reigning down blows on the boy. Julian desperately tries to block the first few punches, but a right hand gets through, dazing him, allowing Michael to begin unloading punches on his defenseless opponent, hitting him at least 30 times before he is knocked out and then hits him at least 20 more, the bones in the boy's faces cracking and breaking as his eye sockets are shattered, cheeks bones are pulverized and teeth are sent dancing across the concrete floor. Each punch is accompanied by an animalistic growl. Julian has always been the weakest of the three and it has been obvious that he would not make it.

Breathing hard, Michael finally stands up, the blood of his opponent dripping from his fists. He did as he has been instructed. In a combat situation, showing mercy is not tolerated. With no emotion, Michael then walks over, takes the plate of food, carries it over to the corner of the room, sits down and begins eating with his bloody hands like an animal. He could take both plates, he has earned them. But he is obedient to orders. One person, one plate. He has learned that not following orders will be met with swift and terrible punishment. So even in this primal state, he follows orders, which is exactly what his instructors had hoped to see.

It takes a few minutes for Kenneth to regain consciousness, but when he does, he sees Julian laying on the floor. He is dead. Kenneth struggles to his feet, takes a look at Michael who is nearly finished with his food, then goes over, takes the second plate of food and begins eating it as fast as he can because he doesn't know how much of the 10 minutes has elapsed.

Friedrich nods his head in approval to Johan. Commander Schmidt will be pleased with this test as Michael has shown promise. Julian's body will be ground up and thrown into der KerKer. As for Kenneth, it is likely that he will not survive the training either, but for now, he has shown enough to be permitted to remain. It is clear to the trainers that Michael is the only one who has a possibility of one day being a Legion member. He has much training still to do, but he has shown promise.

CHAPTER THIRTY-TWO

In his chambers, in an adjacent corridor to the Ark, Tod sits at an old, wooden desk, in silent contemplation, a single candle burning in his sparsely decorated quarters. He sits looking at his hands, running his fingers across the multitude of burn scars on his palms, knuckles and fingers. The room is very plain with dark, wooden walls, a matching ceiling and gray, concrete floor. In addition to the wooden desk with matching wooden chair, the only other furniture is a single bed and one, dark wooden dresser, and one wall with a decorative, red blanket with the all-too-familiar logo that is completely out of place in the plain room, hanging on it. The blanket holds no meaning for him as it does to those other two fools but was simply put up out of necessity.

Both Conrad and Stephan, who have been friends since grammar school and whose positions were secured here decades ago thanks to their fathers, have opted for nicer amenities that are reserved for members of council. Those suites have multiple rooms, with large bathrooms, soft sheets and televisions with a variety of films to choose from. Originally, there were five members of council, but now, all that remain are three.

Tod was offered one of the eight available suites outside of the town but opted for a room with meager accommodations instead. He told the others that he chooses not to be a glutton, instead using only what he needs. It's an attitude that the other four members of council took as pompous, but now only two remain and they have long since quit caring about where Tod chooses to live.

It's a lifestyle that he believes helps cleanse his mind and allows him clarity of thought. For a man who desires little in the way of provisions, where he lays his head is of no concern to him. In addition to his living accommodations, his simple diet consists of whole wheat breads, eggs, Portobello mushrooms, and certain nuts. A specialized diet for a special man.

Conrad and Stephan, both privileged members of this sanctuary, feed their urges through exotic food and both regularly use alcohol, which is illegal in the Ark. Tod is also well aware of their extracurricular activities that include carnal relations with half-breeds from the lower level. It's a disgusting activity that makes Tod want to retch.

Conrad has a weakness for young women from lesser races, sending out his most trusted soldier with the specific purpose of bringing back women of certain descriptions. His appetite for laying with mongrels is against everything the Ark stands for. When they are captured, they are immediately locked in the lower levels, bathed, cleaned and brought to his quarters when he feels the urge. They will never see the Ark, but they also can avoid der Kerker if they cooperate.

Stephan is worse, if that's even possible. He has a liking for young boys. He fulfills his sickening urges as a violent predator that needs his subjects to suffer in order to perform. Tod thinks both will be better off dead.

The two bonded early in life, originally through their fathers who were powerful proponents of the movement. As the got older, they discovered a shared depravity. With neither man being particularly gifted with looks or sexual prowess, both lacked confidence in dating when they attended school, followed by university together. For both, who had few other friends, it began on the outside and more than once their influential fathers saved them from facing legal action. Both were able to squirm their way out of allegations with deep pockets that could buy silence.

When the skies went dark, for a time both found themselves cutoff from the prey they craved. They dare not violate any member of the Ark for they would surely be caught. But eventually, they found ways to feed their desires in the Ark thanks to some mindless automatons in the Legion who will obey orders without question. Since those they violate are not pure, both are able to justify their actions. After all, they aren't really people, just inferior races who have no more rights than a pig that is about to be slaughtered. In fact, both believe they are doing these lesser beings a favor. They are kept out of der Kerker, given food and a clean place to sleep. They should be thanking them.

Both think nobody else knows about their disgusting activities, always trying to present themselves as stern, God-fearing men.

But to Tod, their actions are inconsequential. What does he care what these fools do? After all, now that this plan has been set in motion, nothing can be done to alter the outcome. So, if these buffoons wish to waste their remaining years with such folly, all the better. In fact, their preoccupation with feeding their lust keeps them out of his way.

Three hard knocks on the thick, wooden door rouse Tod from his meditative state. He rises from the chair, adjusts his shirt and tie, and answers the door. He is greeted by a small, squirrelly looking man with blonde hair and green, squinty eyes. Wearing a white, short-sleeved shirt and black, pleated pants, the man gives Tod that customary salute, which he ignores as he walks past him. Tod dismisses the man and walks alone down a series of short, cinderblock hallways until he reaches the area that houses the suites, where abruptly the décor improves tenfold. He moves past the armed guards, giving a curt nod to each as he moves unimpeded for the daily meeting. As he reaches the conference room, highlighted by double doors that are 10 feet high, made of the finest mahogany and adorned with brass handles that are absurd in their fancy design, he enters the space where Conrad and Stephan are already seated at the round table built for five, but now with only three chairs.

Tod nearly rolls his eyes at the torches on the adorned, stone walls that are always lit for daily meetings. Almost nearly as ridiculous to Tod are the banners hanging on each wall emblazoned with the Nazi symbol. Both Conrad and Stephan snap to attention and offer the customary salute. Half-heartedly, Tod returns the gesture before taking his seat to begin the meeting.

While these halfwits believe they serve an important function to this facility, Tod knows better. He is well aware of their unimportance and has to fight the urge to scowl every time he's in their presence as they pompously pontificate about the importance of their mission and how this cleansing process will be looked upon favorably by God. Such antiquated notions are lost on Tod who quietly watches with disgust as these two romanticize about 1940s Germany in a way that simply isn't true. For years, Tod has humored these two only because they pose no real threat. The other two were smart, less self-indulgent, and needed to be removed because they could have caused problems. With Tod's keen intellect and cunning, he was able to remove the other two without raising any suspicion. But Stephan and Conrad lived sheltered lives on the outside and therefore have no real awareness about what is going on around them, making them more of an annoyance to Tod, nothing more. If he eliminated them as well, it would have raised too much suspicion. For that reason, and that reason alone, they continue their roles here for a little while longer.

AUDIO 6

The Nazi party was poised for greatness, but the world didn't agree with that agenda. In the end, the Nazi's were defeated, but not before nearly taking over the world. It's hard to believe how short the memory of people is. After all, the movement was swift and grew exponentially. Much of Europe was conquered and controlled in a short amount of time. Every country on Earth felt the very real possibility of an invasion that would put the Germans as the governing body of the planet. Those who subscribed to the Aryan race believed to be chosen people of perfection.

The Nazi party wanted to take over the world and as they grew in power, that possibility became intoxicating to those who subscribed to such a notion. But in the end, the Nazi party fell, but not without significant damage that carved a scar on the planet that would never fully heal. The defeat was crushing to the party but did the world really think something as powerful as that would go away without a fight? The thought that they would simply crawl in a hole and die was incredibly shortsighted. But that's what it seemed like and that's exactly what our people wanted. To go away without a peep, erasing our near takeover from their minds, allowing us to move forward with this, our next and final plan.

The purification of the world knows no timetable. Ultimately, whether it happened in the 1940s or five generations later, the goal for our people was unwavering. As defeat looked imminent, a new plan was put in place, one that would ensure our victory. One way or another, the endgame was clear. We would cleanse the Earth and allow it to be reborn, free of the half-breed mongrels that polluted the world. The Master Race would reign supreme. That was, and always has been, the end game.

And that foolish and misguided ideal has destroyed the world.

CHAPTER THIRTY-THREE

Clark and Lydia were seated at a small table in a rustic restaurant with walls adorned with black and white photos of musicians playing a variety of instruments. Dinner was mesmerizing for Lydia as men and women in crisp, white shirts with black pants and ties attended to their every need. It seemed that every time Lydia took a sip of water, a young woman would refill the glass with the coldest and best-tasting water she had ever had. It seems like just yesterday that Clark would have to boil dirty water in an old pot over a fire before she could get a drink. He said he had to boil it to make it safe to drink, and it was always cloudy and dirty. How different this wondrous place is.

A man sat at a large, black box with ornate, wooden legs. It was what Clark explained is known as a piano. As she craned her neck to see, one of the waiters encouraged her to walk over to watch him play. She was amazed at watching this young man play, his fingers expertly pushing white and black buttons that sprung the instrument to life. She watched him for more than 10 minutes. At one point, in-between songs, the musician even let Lydia sit down beside him. He then taught her something called chopsticks. After a few tries, she played the tune perfectly, getting a round of applause from the other diners.

When the food arrived, Clark called her back over, his face beaming at the experiences she was getting to receive. The flavors on her plate exploded with each bite as she enjoyed something called spaghetti.

She also got the opportunity to try out a few bites of Clark's meal too. He had something called fish tacos, which Clark said was a favorite of his as a boy. It too tasted delicious to her. The wonders of this place were unceasing, and she still was having difficulty believing that it was real. She looked around the room, seeing tables full of smiling people eating more varieties of food than she ever knew existed.

Just when she thought things couldn't get better, it was a dish called dessert that made the day perfect. She was served something called a Chocolate Sundae. It is by far the best thing she has ever eaten in her short life. The decadent, rich flavors tantalized her taste buds to the point where she actually let out a smiling groan after her first bite that made Clark laugh heartily. Lydia examined his face during this, having never seen this emotion from him. She liked it a lot.

Following diner, Lydia's belly felt stretched out, an uncomfortable yet satisfying sensation. Clark suggested a walk to help them digest their meals, so they strolled through the streets for a while, followed by sitting on a bench with some others at the end of town, watching a spectacular sunset, complete with a few shooting stars. A perfect ending to a perfect day.

This place is an oasis, full of pleasure and excitement. She almost forgot what it was like to have sadness, fear and pain. That is until later that night when she woke in the middle of night, vomiting and in severe stomach pain. Clark immediately tended to her and correctly suspected what was happening. While he could have called the hospital to have orderlies rush to their apartment to get her, Clark elected to carry the small, cramping child to the hospital. It was there that the night doctor ordered imaging tests to discover that Lydia was suffering from appendicitis. The technician even showed Clark the image on a handheld computer and was told that it is fortunate they caught it now as the appendix was expanded and on the verge of perforating. If that had happened while on the outside, it would've been a death sentence.

Fortunately, the doctor explained that he only needed to make three, small hole-shaped incisions and the appendix can be safely removed. She will only need to spend one or two days in the hospital. Clark breathes a sigh of relief that what occurred is so minor.

Clark sits with her inside the small examining room, the familiar scent of disinfectant reminding him of his days working in hospitals. He has dimmed the lights so she can rest, having calmly explained the situation to Lydia, assuring her that all would be fine. Unlike most hospitals in the old world where every procedure took forever to prepare for as they were notorious for working at a glacial pace, here in the Ark, with everybody living close by and having tasks to perform, the operating room was prepared in about two hours. Clark kisses her on the forehead as they wheel her into the O.R. for a minor surgery that would only take about an hour.

CHAPTER THIRTY-FOUR

Mason's increased immune function, enhanced vision and physical training are unmatched. Through the years, others who showed promise were put through similar training and improvement procedures, but none could come close to his level. Other than his propensity to show mercy, he is a nearly perfect weapon. In fact, the only thing about him that requires any maintenance at all are his cochlear implants that allow him hearing that is better than most canines. These require being recharged a few times a year, which necessitates a small procedure where a tiny, camera-guided instrument is inserted into the ear canal where a charging port allows them to be recharged.

Ben used to handle these sessions. In fact, since the implants were installed, nobody other than Ben has ever done it. But now that he's gone, Rachel has been tasked with the duty. While she is much prettier than Ben, for Mason, who had developed a bond with the aging physician, it's a stark reminder of the void left in his life now that Ben is gone. While Mason has long ago learned how to suppress his emotions, he would be lying if he told himself that he doesn't miss Ben.

In all fairness, Mason dislikes these sessions no matter who is doing them. It's not that it hurts, because pain is something he has learned to turn off like a switch. It's more of an uncomfortable feeling, like bees in his ears as the tiny batteries are given their charge. Perhaps he dislikes it because it is something he can't control.

Rachel and Mason are comfortable together. In a different world, who knows, Mason wonders if they could have had a relationship. In truth, Mason knows nothing about what a real relationship would entail. He has had a few flings with a couple young ladies over the years, but nothing that he would call serious. He's caught Rachel starring at him over the years, and she has recognized that he too is attracted to her. But she's very serious about her duties here in the Ark, and Mason doesn't exactly live a normal life. In fact, he knows that it wouldn't be fair to ever have a relationship considering that during his missions on the outside he could be killed. Whoever was unlucky enough to be with him would spend weeks on end dreading the unknown, always wondering if he would return. If he ever could have a normal life, he definitely thinks he and Rachel would be a perfect fit. But there's no use in thinking about that, not considering his role in the Ark.

He does wonder what kind of father he would have made. The closest thing he has ever experienced would be his mentor role in training young Legion members. But he suspects that raising a child would be largely different. Not that it matters, as all births here in the Ark must be approved ahead of time and are carefully monitored. Mason has never been authorized for procreation and if he ever is, it would likely be due to his prowess as a soldier and would be just to create a prospective Legion member. While he doesn't regret his life, he doubts very much that he would ever want to put his potential offspring through the training necessary to attain that status.

With the right ear out of the way, Mason sits patiently as Rachel begins the procedure for the left ear. Everything goes normally as the charging port slides perfectly into the cochlear port. Then … all hell breaks loose.

A symphony of sounds erupts and Mason grimaces in agony as the cacophony of noise bombards him. Nothing like this has ever happened before and the pain is so bad that his vision blurs for a few moments. Rachel grabs his arm, and he can see that she is trying to talk to him, but he cannot hear anything over the screeching sound that is assaulting his senses. But then the noise slowly fades away and then there is something else. Something unexpected. Ben's voice takes over.

AUDIO 1:

"Listen to me very carefully, Mason. I am going to explain everything to you."

CHAPTER THIRTY-FIVE

Tod strolls into what looks like an airplane hangar. It's a massive space with fluorescent lights humming, basking the concrete space in a bluish hue. Three men in lab coats immediately snap to attention when they see him.

Behind them are all three, metallic, gleaming rockets, each more than eight meters tall. Tod smiles as he looks at them, their shape and size looking delightfully foreboding. He strolls around each rocket, not really examining them, more like admiring each before turning back to the men.

"Report?"

"Inspections are done. Everything is completed."

"And the delivery system? Tod asks.

"It took some effort. We had to fabricate it to fit your request from scratch."

"Show me."

The first man snaps his fingers and the other two engineers rush into action with one going to a computer console and the other to one of the rockets. Tod and the main engineer move closer to get a better look.

"This is all so very exciting sir. Do you really believe we can heal the planet?"

"Dr. Dunmire, what we are going to do will fix this world once and for all."

"I'm so proud to be part of this."

"As you should be."

Dr. Dunmire, the engineer in charge begins the rudimentary explanation of how each rocket will be programmed to travel to the specified altitude and locations and then the hatch will open and the substance Tod supplies will be delivered. They watch as the hatch opens, revealing the canisters. Dr. Dunmire's heart swells with pride as Tod smiles. While Tod expects that just one will do the job, he doesn't want to leave anything to chance. Not now. Not after all of his careful planning.

"You and your team have done an amazing job. You should be very proud."

"Thank you, may I ask a question?"

"Of course."

"Why are we keeping this miraculous world cure a secret?"

"Because even though I am supremely confident that this will work, I don't want to raise everybody's hopes until after the launch and we can do some measurements of the outside world."

"Of course. That makes sense."

"While I am optimistic that this will indeed cure our wounded world, the psychological component of hope is tricky. The last thing we want is for our beloved citizens to get hopeful of returning to our world soon, only to be let down."

"Understandable, sir," Dunmire says.

"But don't worry, you will each get full credit for your role in finally healing our fractured world once and for all."

"It has been our supreme honor to be part of this."

"Well done indeed," Tod shouts to the other two men who also smile and snap out salutes. "You will be remembered throughout history for your contributions."

Tod spins on his heels and abruptly walks out of the space, the three engineers who have been sworn to secrecy, beaming at the compliment and thrilled at the concept that they will play a key role in expediting the Earth's removal from the darkness so that the occupants of the Ark can emerge from the subterranean in months rather than decades according to Tod's explanation of how they will heal the planet by seeding the atmosphere with a compound that will hasten the world's emergence from this winter. A lie.

Tod still wears a smile as he navigates the empty, industrial hallways, its steel pipes providing much of the lifeblood to the Ark in the form of clean water, oxygen and heat. Something he could halt in an instance if and when he chooses. The power he holds is intoxicating. It is God-like.

Using a thick, small towel that he always keeps folded in his pocket, he pulls the metal door handle, opening the large, gray door. He enters a room full of monitors and with a few key strikes he finds the footage he is looking for. Motion activated, these cameras in this subterranean part of the facility only activate when there are people in areas where they shouldn't be. Tod is the only one who has access to it. Hidden, disguised as light fixtures, Tod is able to see all and know all. What he sees is troubling, causing his smile to evaporate. What is Rachel doing in an unauthorized area with Vance? This will have to be remedied. Even though the microphones cannot pick up their hushed conversation due to all the noise from the river, what they are meeting about is clear. Vance has become chatty it would seem. Something that isn't terribly surprising as Vance, while brilliant, is a bit of a nervous coward.

But it is all inconsequential at this point. The plan has been executed to perfection and the conclusion is finally at hand. Decades of planning, of playing the game, acting in a role, will all be worth it.

CHAPTER THIRTY-SIX

The misery of der Kerker is by design. Dark and dank, it is a place built for the specific purpose of suffering. This long, cylinder-shaped space has been carved out of the stone walls. More than 100 meters long, but just 40 meters wide, more than 400 poor souls of every lesser race reside in this hell on Earth. Many were brought here before it all happened, for the alleged purpose of study and experimentation, the rest have been brought by a select few Legion members who had a predilection for violence and anger at an early age and therefore were conditioned since they were infants to serve this cause. But the real reason is much more sinister. It's to create a place for suffering. A hell on Earth.

While Mason, Gibby and a few others are sent out to find people or resources to help the world, the others are given much darker tasks. They are sent out to bring back a specific type of person or people. Their reward, aside from extra rations and other amenities, is that they are tasked with slaughtering everybody else they meet. It is engrained in them and they don't know anything else. They simply follow orders to the letter, never deviating from the mission, unlike Mason who has a knack for revising plans at times.

Tod walks to a small, hidden window high above der Kerker, where he enjoys looking in and seeing the suffering. He thinks to himself that Vance will reside here by the end of the day. The floor is covered in feces, bile and urine. The strong one's sleep sitting up, while the weak often pass out with their heads and faces in the waste. Many are moaning in a haze from fever as their bodies fight infection, others occasionally die. But the goal is to give them just enough to stay alive, but not to live. Nobody has ever been removed from this space, it's a one-way trip. Allowing anybody to leave for any reason would create hope, and hope is the enemy. So instead, they remain, forced to live with decomposing corpses of those who perished.

A tiny bit of water trickles down the far wall continuously. It is the only water in the space and the occupants put their mouths on the stone walls to suck and lick it up to quench their thirst. As with everything else in this hellhole, there is just enough to stay alive.

Tod watches as the far hatch opens and leftover scraps are poured into the space, splashing on the disgusting, rock floor. The meat has been ground up and is a combination of tilapia leftovers as well as a young boy who didn't survive his training. They would likely not eat it if they knew some of the meat was human, which is why it was ground up.

Tod wants to watch the strong ones climb over each other to get a couple handfuls of food, often just scraps that, in addition to the little bit of ground meat, include a variety of fruits and vegetables that either spoiled or were partially eaten. He frowns when he doesn't get his wish.

Many of these people who are strong enough to get to the food take what they can secure and give it to others who are unable to fight for it. That irritates him because it shows they still have some humanity left. He would like nothing more than to see them transformed into mindless animals with no regard for each other. He shows particular disgust as he sees a few of these people actually fold their hands and close their eyes before eating. Praying to some deity that their mongrel nations have created over the centuries angers him because it shows that some still harbor hope. Hope, above all else, is what he would like to see squashed. Because once hope is gone, true suffering can reach its zenith.

Tod eventually exits the observation area, travels through a few, short hallways, and enters a secondary chamber. In here, behind barred cells, he walks through the desolate space. While it is stark and bare, it's clean and the occupants are one to a cell and each has a working toilet, sink and small cot. All have been bathed and disinfected. They should enjoy it while they can because when all this is completed, these pets of Stephan and Conrad will also be cast into der Kerker with the others. For now, to occupy those two morons, Tod allows it. After all, he has needed them over the years because they enjoy mingling with the occupants, regularly strolling through the Ark, smugly enjoying how the inhabitants regard them regally. Tod hates being around these primates, of which he is technically a member. So, he only appears when necessary, putting on the show of the warm, cuddly grandfather when he'd like nothing better than to rip out their beating hearts and show it to them.

It amuses him how Conrad, Stephan and the other members of council falsely believe they are finishing the somehow divine work of a madman who died before any of them were even born. None of them know the truth. That it is he and he alone who has orchestrated all that is, and all that ever will be, on this gloomy rock.

CHAPTER THIRTY-SEVEN

Clark spent much of the next few days despondent, in a painful haze following Lydia's death.

He had sat in the waiting room, anxiously waiting for the nurse to emerge with a smile, telling him everything went well and that he could go and see her. The pang of dread he felt when instead the doctor emerged with a pained look on his face is hard to quantify. The surgeon sat and explained to the doctor about the adverse reaction Lydia had to the anesthesia.

While in a daze, Clark half listened to the explanation from the surgeon about an inherited abnormality that caused a severe reaction to the anesthesia that caused malignant hyperthermia. Typically, there is a family history of sensitivity to anesthesia, and in such cases, they can do a different procedure, such as a spinal block so the patient can have the surgery without being put under. But since there is no record of the girl's family history because she was born after the war, they had no way of knowing that she carried this extremely rare trait.

Clark insisted on seeing her, wanting to look at her with his own eyes, perhaps hoping there was some mistake. But upon seeing her lifeless face, her little body which was so happy just a few hours ago, now without a pulse, he crumbled to the floor. After all she lived through, all of the horror she saw, he could have never imagined her dying like this. He feels the impact even harder because he finally let his guard down. On the outside, he was always prepared for the fact that death loomed around every corner. Each day, losing their lives was a very real possibility. But when they arrived in the Ark and saw all it had to offer, he actually believed for the first time since it all started that perhaps someday, they … she could have had a real life. She was placed in a small coffin, outside of town, where Ben and a few others who have departed are kept, with the promise of a proper burial someday when they emerge from underground. Clark spent hours with her, sitting beside the box, weeping. Finally, he was convinced to go home.

After her death, he spent days in the apartment, not really eating, in mourning. A grief counselor visited him daily, as did Rachel and a few others to offer condolences. Clark sat in her bedroom, looking at her clothing, or going through some of her drawings as she was recently introduced to crayons. Nearly ever picture she drew is of he and her, smiling.

Finally, he wills himself out of the apartment, the only real home Lydia ever knew, to walk to the hospital after Rachel sent word that she desperately needed his consultation about a patient. While the last thing he feels like doing is leaving the apartment, he knows that as a doctor he took an oath to help whenever he is called upon. Upon entering the hospital, Rachel hugs him, squeezing him hard, tears in her eyes. At first, he is rigid and unmoving, but slowly, he hugs her back, allowing himself a sobby embrace with her. After a few moments, she asks him to come and check on a patient. He obediently follows her, willing his body to move as nearly unbearable sorrow threatens to overtake him. He enters the darkened room as Rachel swings the heavy, metal door closed with a thud. It takes a few moments for his eyes to adjust to the slightest of illumination caused by the dials on the Magnetic Resonance Imaging machine. He can see another figure in the room, in the corner in the shadows. The figure moves toward him. It's Mason.

Shrouded in darkness, the low hum of the MRI system the only sound, Rachel puts her hand on Clark's shoulder and begins speaking in hushed tones.

"This is the only room I have authorization to that I'm certain doesn't have cameras or microphones. The electromagnets will blow out any electronic surveillance."

"What are you talking about? Why are we in here?"

"Clark. This place is not what it seems. They hear all and know all."

"Who?"

"What I know for sure is that we cannot trust anybody."

"I'm very confused right now."

"Clark. Listen," she continues. "What happened to Lydia … I'm so sorry. But I don't believe it was an accident."

"What?" he nearly shouts, getting a shush from Rachel.

"What she means is that she was murdered," Mason offers, his delivery even and measured.

"Murdered?"

"Over the years, Mason has brought back people like yourself. An engineer, mechanic, botanist, and others that fit a specific profile. On more than one occasion he has been chastised for bringing back somebody that didn't fit the list of essential personnel."

"Essential personnel?"

"Sometimes, I find somebody who is not alone. They have a wife or partner, maybe a child or close friend. Knowing they won't willingly leave somebody behind I sometimes made the decision to bring them along."

"Like Lydia?"

"Like Lydia," Rachel explains.

"What is wrong with that?" Clark asks." She's just one little girl. There is plenty of space and resources."

"It's not really about that," Rachel says. "It's about the bloodline."

"Bloodline?"

"Yes." Rachel continues. "You, me and Mason have a bloodline that can be traced back centuries. We are all from the same lineage. One that is sought to be above all others."

"Wait. What?"

"A bloodline that is considered pure."

"Are you talking about the Aryan Nation?"

Rachel pauses for a moment, allowing Clark to absorb all of this.

"Your expertise is important, but you also have another critical component. Your DNA. The research team discovered a high likelihood that you were of the pure race. That's why Mason was told to bring you in. But Lydia's blood test was considered unclean."

"So, you killed her?" Clark says with a sob.

"No," Mason says firmly. "We did no such thing. They did it."

"While I have no proof, I believe she was intentionally given something during her meal that caused her severe stomach pain. Then, when brought into the hospital, I believe they falsely made a diagnosis of appendicitis so she could be put under."

"And then, what? Murder her? She was just a little girl," Clark says as he puts his hand on a wall for support.

"That's what I'm telling you. Over the years, anybody who Mason has brought back without the right DNA has met with an unfortunate ending."

Mason picks up the narrative, his delivery even and serious.

"A man was sent to work in an area where the turbines are and within a month, his safety harness failed and he fell into the raging river below."

"A woman who Mason brought back with her pure blood husband ended up dying from anaphylactic shock after eating some chestnuts only a few weeks after being here," Rachel explains.

"What kind of place is this?" Clark asks.

"Originally, it was supposed to be a place where a certain set of people could live together in harmony, awaiting a time when the world was safe to re-enter," Rachel says. "I believed it for a long time. But I don't anymore and neither does Mason. We once thought this to be a haven."

"And now?" Clark asks.

“Hell!” Mason sternly says.

AUDIO 7:

Led by a charismatic man who people would follow blindly, some called him a genius, others a madman. The Fuhrer was a proponent of the quest for genetic perfection. Because of that he allocated untold resources to the science that is the human body. Undocumented and untold atrocities were committed by Nazi doctors on human beings of all races through experiments that are almost too gruesome to imagine. Due to having no regard for humanity, Germans were way ahead of other nations in this field. They were able to push boundaries that nobody else could because they had no regard for their subjects.

When World War II began to wind down and a loss for the Nazi party was imminent, a contingency plan was put in place. The Nazi leader believed he was of divine creation and therefore his existence was beyond that of any ordinary man. He did not believe he could die. At least not permanently.

All parts of his DNA, tissue, blood, even bone marrow was harvested in the months leading up to his death. That DNA was stored until such time that German scientists perfected a procedure that would allow him to retake his rightful place.

Sadly, I was part of the team that successfully cloned the Fuhrer and breathed life back into him. He believed that when he was reborn, he would return to power. He felt his divine spirit, his very soul would return. The plan was to groom him from birth to retake his throne as it were. He was certain he had God-like ability and when he was reborn, he would reclaim his throne.

In the first decade of his life, it looked promising as he seamlessly adjusted to and accepted his destiny. In fact, it was almost eerie how quickly he took to his role. But soon it became apparent that while he was identical to his doppelganger in physical appearance, it was his intellect where the difference was noticeable. While the original was well above average in intelligence, the replacement had cognitive abilities that were beyond anything anybody had ever seen before. He absorbed knowledge at an exponential rate, soon surpassing that of his educators. By the time he was 20, he was likely the smartest being who ever existed.

While he excelled in every subject, he had a specific gift for science, something the original also enjoyed but had limited understanding of. It was he who was one of the primary members of the team that created the virus as part of a plan to wipe the world clean. He created the highly contagious, two-part disease to clean the slate. And it worked. He also helped create the inoculation that was given to those chosen for life in the Ark.

All was going according to plan until recently. You see, the Fuhrer has a completely different look now. Other than me, his true origins are a secret. Even the other council members do not now who, or what he truly is. It was his belief that his true identity was to be kept a secret until the time was right, as he explained it. His appearance has been altered with two, small procedures and with his shaggy hair and full beard, he is disguised, but Tod is that clone and I fear that our original plan to cleanse the world is not his plan. In fact, the man we created in a test tube, the being that we believed would be our savior, actually wants nothing more than to extend human suffering. He is not who he was.

What we wanted to recreate was Adolf Hitler. What we got was something much, much worse.

CHAPTER THIRTY-EIGHT

Tod despises the weakness of this body as he can feel it breaking down, knowing he will need the procedure done soon. Being a superior being in this feeble form, scurrying around like a rodent is nearly intolerable to him. But it's better than the alternative, existing alone as a mere apparition, a lifetime of otherworldly knowledge but powerless to do anything other than observe.

Throughout history, beings like it have been called demons, jinns, imps and dybbuks. Each culture or religion gave them a different designation.

Having existed since the beginning, entering the body of some unsuspecting human for a few minutes, hours or even days before bouncing to another, it was an opportunity to experience life. But for Tod, he wasn't satisfied with just watching. When somebody would think to themselves, "what made me say that" or "what made me do that," it was the work of Tod or a few others like it. The duration they are able to stay in a person varies from human to human depending on certain biological factors. In fact, when they enter a body, it causes no harm to the human. The people don't even realize when these beings are riding along. The only side-effect is that whatever the human is doing at the time causes a memory echo. Sometimes it will make the person stop what they are doing for a moment, often shaking their head or remarking about the strange feeling to another. These humans call this déjà vu. Before the world fell into chaos, these feelings were only occasional since there were billions of humans to choose from and only a fraction as many of these beings. But now, since these beings will not bond with those who are suffering, they all must wait their turn to enter those in the Ark who are living happy and satisfying lives. It has caused great disharmony with these beings for whom joining with humans has been a major part of their existence for thousands and thousands of years. It has been a symbiotic relationship that has shaped their very culture.

Since this déjà vu feeling happens to everybody from time-to-time, they all largely ignore it and keep on with their lives without skipping a beat. It's only a new experience for recent arrivals, like Clark and Lydia. And even they already began to adjust to the experience.

From inside these lesser beings, for the one that became Tod, the thrill was in creating pain and suffering. Whether it was orchestrating acts to destroy a friendship or causes an argument, it was the only existence it ever knew, bouncing back and forth from its home in the Realm with others of its kind, to the physical world. While most of the individuals from this race opt for a peaceful union with humans, satisfied to ride along and experience life for a short time, a few, like Tod, discovered that with some practice, they could actually influence these humans, where they would say or do something they didn't really mean. While a small number opted to become influencers of this race, over the years a few did real damage until these beings finally took a stand.

But Tod's biggest mistake happened more than a millennium ago when it entered a teenage girl of a prominent family in an area that we now call Turkey. Using all of its otherworldly cunning, it used deception and sex to tear the family apart. While there wasn't a medical name for it back then, the girl suffered from severe anemia and something about her physiology allowed him to stay in her much longer than any other human he had bonded with before. This was something that had never occurred before and the extended time allowed Tod to go from simply influencing the girl, to totally control her and to create chaos. But it didn't anticipate what came next.

A family of devout faith, they suspected something was terribly wrong with their daughter due to her erratic behavior. A religious leader of unequalled ability was brought in, disguised as a servant, where he gave the girl a sleeping potion. The man suspected the girl was possessed, so he did everything secretly, keeping his intentions veiled. Tod and his race very much enjoy the experience of sleeping, something that doesn't exist in the Realm. So, Tod allowed himself to drift off, enjoying the restful dreams of his human host. But when he awoke, he discovered he was tied down with iron bindings while also covered in various medallions, coins and a metallic dust.

Knowing it was caught, the creature that would become Tod tried in vain to escape the girl but was unable to break away. Normally, he could leave a human at will, but in this situation, for the first time in its existence, it was stuck. Through a cadence it never heard before, it was subject to agonizing pain for the first time. The suffering was unlike anything it ever knew. It's entire being felt as though it was being boiled.

The one who would become Tod felt rage that was palpable as this foolish religious man mumbled chants, trying to vanquish some imagined demon or devil from the girl. Tod can't believe he allowed himself to be caught in this manner. To make matters worse, it watched as others like it, entered and exited the religious zealot over a matter of days, gleeful and happy as they disapproved of Tod's actions and celebrated his torture. It infuriated him.

Finally, after days of suffering, it was expelled from the sweating girl who was screaming in pain throughout the duration of this exorcism of sorts, but instead of being hurled back to its Realm, it simply stayed. At first it was unsettling, but hardly anything it couldn't overcome. After all, it was clearly weakened from the experience and was likely just disorientated. The real terror didn't take hold until it realized the man not only exorcised it, he somehow warded it from ever possessing a body with a soul again, but also from ever moving on. For the first few days, it truly expected that at any moment, it would be snapped back into the Realm, but that never happened. It attempted to re-enter other humans for many years, with no success. It simply could no longer enter or join. So, all it could do was wiggle around the physical world, an invisible bystander. While it didn't see with eyes, as it does when in a body, it does sense all that is going on around it, the population growing exponentially, spreading to every corner of the world.

In the Realm, time doesn't really exist, but when in the physical world, it feels every second of every day in real time. With nothing to do but watch, weeks stretched into months, then years and decades, time slowly passing, an intolerable purgatory. And that had been its existence for nearly 1,300 years. Drifting aimlessly, unable to do anything other than observe, it was maddening. It would have welcomed death, something it and its kind do not have the privilege to experience. Infinite suffering with no end.

In limbo, it watched the rise and crumble of dynasties, even able to sense others like it entering humans and enjoying the life it once knew. Over the centuries, fear turned to sorrow, followed by frustration, then madness, and ultimately evolving into an all-consuming, burning hate. Hatred for these apes that he used to manipulate like puppets as well as for the others like it. Its own kind saw its plight, but since they disapproved of its damaging actions on the humans over countless millenniums', none ever acknowledged it. They simply soared past, entering and exiting humans, bouncing between worlds, learning and experiencing while it could do nothing but watch.

It took centuries for these primates to finally do anything of real consequence, but when they created the perfect host, it finally had respite. After endlessly squirming around in the physical world as a silent, powerless observer, simply watching in complete solitude, it discovered something different, something unnatural. It was hard to quantify. Over the years, before its exile, these beings could sense a glow in humans who were unoccupied. Using it like a beacon, they could join with this power source, instantly bonding with the body. That same glow now repels it any time it gets close.

But then it sensed something different. A being with a void, unlike anything it had ever felt before.

The warding placed upon it all those years ago kept it from possessing anybody with a soul, something all beings, young, old and even dead have or had. But for the first time, a being existed that was born soulless. The being that would become known as Tod entered this lifeless shell, immediately animating it. But like before, soon he would weaken and get expelled from the body, but instead of going back to the Realm, it would remain, hovering over the body. After a matter of hours, it would regain its strength and would be able to re-enter for a while, with the same thing happening over and over.

That was the pattern, but he was unwilling to give up. Not after spending 13 centuries alone. Thankfully, Ben finally figured out a treatment, then refined it a few times, resulting in the existence that Tod now enjoys. It's not ideal, but compared to floating alone for eternity, it has sufficed.

Now they will pay. These humans as well as his own race. All of them will pay for what they did to him. When the plan is done, the Earth will be void of all life and all that will remain will be der Kerker. Those who left him to his eternal existence will all suffer now. Currently, its own race, which has a static number that never changes and he estimates to be a couple hundred thousand, must share rides with the few hundred living in the Ark. But soon, the others like it will have no hosts other than those living in their own filth in der Kerker. Their only options will be the blankness of the Realm, or to share the misery of the humans they enter. Now that their race has come to thrive on experiences, both options will be nothing but misery. It will drive them mad, too.

CHAPTER THIRTY-NINE

Still reeling from the loss of Lydia, and now working with purpose, Clark begins working shifts in the hospital, even getting a visit from Stephan who offers his sincerest condolences on her death. Clark does his best to hide his anger, instead discussing his work with Stephan. He purposely talks in medical jargon, watching as Stephan happily nods his head in agreement, even though he has no idea what he's hearing.

Regardless, Stephan is happy to have Clark on board, doing whatever work is needed. After all, he is a brilliant scientist who will add to the perfection that is the Ark. Rachel has been instructed to see that he continues any work Ben was doing. Tod is particularly interested in Clark's abilities and has informed all hospital members to make Clark's transition as smooth as possible. At some point, he hopes that Clark's talents will potentially help to refine his secret treatments so he doesn't have to have them done as often.

Stephan strolls out of the hospital feeling downright jubilant. After all, Lydia couldn't be permitted to stay here, her imperfect genes polluting the very air the chosen ones breathe. He was concerned how Clark would respond but is elated with how quickly he has adjusted. She wasn't even his real daughter, so Stephan ponders that perhaps they did Clark a favor. Now he is no longer her charge and he can enjoy the oasis that was created for people like him.

The absurdity of his feeling of superiority is lost on this pompous fool who lived an extraordinarily privileged life on the outside, one that has continued here on the inside. He strolls through the town, happily waving to the citizens as he moves through the community. He even stops to take a knee and do a magic trick with a coin to the elation of a couple of young boys who have no idea that this grandfather-type of man is a twisted pedophile. But it's a double life he has lived for so long that he has become an expert at playing his part.

He's in a particularly good mood because Trevor, his most trusted Legion member, has recently returned and brought back the requested item. Young and relatively healthy, the thought of this supple little, Latino boy causes his lust to grow at the thought, giving him butterflies in his stomach at what he plans to do. It's been a good day. A good day indeed.

Meanwhile, Clark works tirelessly, now motivated by revenge. Mason shared what he learned from Ben with Rachel and Clark. That information combined with the work Vance explained to Rachel has given them a fairly clear vision of what horror is imminent. It is likely that they are the only ones in the facility aware of the evil that guides the Ark. The entire community has been built on a lie. But even Conrad and Stephan are unaware that they too are pawns. While he keeps a low-profile, acting charming and engaging when he must, there has never been anyone like Tod. He is evil incarnate. Now they have recognized where the threat lies.

After putting the puzzle pieces together, they know that the substance called Reinigen, which is German for cleanse, has been synthesized and perfected. If it is released into the oxygen system in the Ark, everybody will suffocate in minutes. But why go through all of the trouble of building the Ark, saving and caring for all these people, only to turn around and kill them? It didn't make sense. That's when the chilling reality hit them. That Tod plans on releasing Reinigen into the world above. If it indeed works like Vance explained to Rachel, then it will grow and divide exponentially until every trace of oxygen on the planet has been absorbed. The Earth will never be habitable again. Is that the endgame that Ben spoke about?

CHAPTER FORTY

Vance is keeping up appearances, continuing to do his normal work, going to the lab to keep doing his experiments. In truth, he has refined Reinigen as much as possible. Lately most of his work has been redundant experiments with conclusions he already knows. But still, that has been his orders, so he goes through the motions.

After walking through the manned security door, still having to submit to hands scans even though he has been the only person for months, other than Tod, to enter, the protocol is always the same. Finally, after being cleared, he enters the lab and his heart skips a beat as he sees Tod sitting in a chair, his hands folded in his lap. Tod offers a big smile to Vance.

"Good morning, Vance."

"Um. Hello sir. I'm sorry, did I miss an appointment with you?"

"Oh, no, no. I just wanted to stop in to check on things. How are you today?"

"I'm. I'm fine. Thank you."

"Are you sure? You seem unsettled," Tod asks. "Is everything alright?"

"Yes. Of course. Everything is fine."

"Good. Very good."

Tod gets up and strolls through the room, his complexion now pale and his movements taking effort. Usually, Tod will not allow others to observe him when he is weakened, but today he doesn't concern himself with outside appearances.

"Your work here has been groundbreaking. You should be very proud of your accomplishments here," Tod says in a sing-song voice, putting Tod's mind at ease.

"Thank you. That means a lot to me."

"The compound you helped create is going to repair this world once and for all. I'm very pleased with your work. Is there anything else you require to take your work further?"

"No sir. In fact, that saturation is at a level that I never thought would be possible," Vance says, now speaking more confidently. "It is now self-sustaining as you know. I believe it has been refined to the point of perfection. I believe that we should begin to concentrate on how to take that stored oxygen, stop its growth, and reverse it so that it can be released."

"Yes. That seems like the next logical step, doesn't it?"

"It does, sir. And I believe it is something we will be able to achieve. In fact, I have created some chemical compound combinations that I believe show promise. Of course, it will take time and experimentation, but I'm confident that …"

"Yes, yes," Tod cuts him off with a dismissing wave of the hand. "I have gone over all of the data and I believe Reinigen is now perfect. So now, I feel that we need to put you on a new project."

"A new project?" Vance says with hesitation. "But we still have work to do on this. Without stabilizing it, we won't be able to engineer it to release the stored oxygen."

"Vance. You need a change of scenery. After all, you have been diligently working on this project for a very long time. And now, I believe you are ready for a new assignment. Isn't that exciting?"

"Yes sir. Uh. Of course. But we aren't done with this one yet. We still need to unlock the stored oxygen. Isn't that the next assignment?"

"You have done a fine job. In fact, I don't believe it could have been done without you. But now, your talents are needed elsewhere."

Tod saunters over and knocks on the lab door. Immediately, Colin enters the space, his eyes cold and dead, sending a shudder through Vance.

"I want you to go with Colin. He will take you to your new project."

Vance doesn't move, frozen with fear.

"I think this new challenge will be … interesting," Tod purrs.

"What is it?"

"I think you'll need to see it to believe it. I feel like it is one of my biggest achievements. One that will benefit from having you be part of it."

Tod moves toward the door, turning before he leaves, his face and voice now different. The jovial tone gone; his eyebrows now furrowed.

"I really do appreciate all that you have done. Consider this your reward."

With that, Tod exits the room and walks down the corridor and disappears through the security door. Vance turns and looks at Colin who offers a sinister smile. Two more Legion members appear in the doorway and Vance fully expects to be killed. But instead, he is aggressively escorted by a Legion member on each arm, with Colin walking behind. He is taken down some dark, concrete stairs into a lower level of the facility that even he never knew existed.

"Where are we going?" Vance asks with a trembling voice.

But nobody answers him. In fact, none of them even speak to him, just pulling and pushing him down the stairs and then into a corridor that smells so bad that he feels he might throw up.

"I need to speak to Tod."

At the end of the concrete corridor, he is stopped where the three begin aggressively tearing at his clothes, ripping them from his body, where in a matter of seconds his pale, skinny body is left shivering and afraid.

"What are you doing? Please stop this!" Vance shrieks with terror in his voice. Vance has always lived a life of privilege and protection, so this is the first time in his life he has ever experienced poor treatment.

"I demand to speak to Conrad immediately," Vance says through tears, causing Colin to laugh, followed by the other two.

All three Legion members step back and look at this small, pathetic excuse for a man. They then all remove thick, heavy black masks from their pockets and put them on. Colin then walks over and opens a big, metal hatch, instantly flooding the space with an ungodly stink. Vance tries to retreat into the corner to evade them, but he is weak and unskilled and is easily corralled by the hulking men. They shove him back and forth, their laughing muffled by their masks. After playing with him like cats with an injured mouse, he is lifted and shoved through the hatch where he tumbles down a metal slide, hearing the hatch slam shut behind him. Is he being dropped into a pit, outside, a grave? His mind doesn't even have time to process it all before he slides through the darkness, dropping out of an opening and plummeting 10 feet, landing in feces, urine, and bile onto a concrete floor. It's dark, but there is just enough light to see as he turns and looks back to watch a second hatch slide shut. His face, mouth and naked body is covered in the slop and he begins vomiting uncontrollably from the worst conditions imaginable. His pampered life did nothing to prepare him for the sudden plunge into horror.

A few people walk over to him, also naked and emaciated, one taking a knee and telling him to try to calm his breathing. But after throwing up, and then dry heaving for a time, he finally must have passed out.

His next memory is waking up, propped against the wall to keep his face out of the filth. One of the others must have put him there. He feels like vomiting again, but does as he was told, taking a few deep breaths, squelching the urge for the moment. He wipes his eyes to view a sea of naked bodies filling the space of some kind of underground dungeon. While he doesn't know the name of this place, he has been cast into der Kerker with untold others, moaning and crying, living in hell on Earth. He immediately begins to sob.

While Vance is of pure bloodline, der Kerker isn't only a place for mongrels and half-breeds from the old world, it will soon be the home for virtually everybody. Now that Vance has outlived his usefulness, this will be his home until the day he dies.

CHAPTER FORTY-ONE

While Mason is a trusted member of the Legion, even he doesn't have unauthorized access to much of the facility. Typically, outside of the Ark, he is relegated to areas where Legion members train. But with what he now knows, his job is clear.

He slides through the hallways, getting pretty far before having to grab one of the technicians and force him to open the hatch to an even deeper level of the facility. It took some time and some degree of arm-twisting, but he finally made it into the hangar that houses the rockets. Vance theorized that Tod must have some sort of delivery system because Reinigen works best when it is airborne. Mason, being aware of the hangar where engineers fabricate needed items, theorized that it would be the ideal location to create a rocket.

But upon entering the space, he quickly realizes it was a trap. To make matters worse, Commander Schmidt, Colin, Trevor, Jonathan, Johan and Friedrich emerge from behind equipment in all corners of the facility, firearms trained on Mason. While Mason has always been the alpha, in truth, Schmidt has been discreetly polluting these Legion members' minds in regard to Mason. Telling them that he breaks orders and doesn't have the best interest of the Ark in mind.

"Hello Mason," Schmidt says with a satisfied smirk on his face.

"What's all this?" Mason says.

"Come now, you didn't really think you made it down here without us knowing? It is obvious you came down here with sabotage on your mind. Did you expect it would be left unprotected?"

"Well. I was kinda hoping," Mason chuckles.

"As unpredictable as you think you are, we know you better than you know yourself. It was easy to predict exactly what you would say or do."

"Feeling good about yourself?"

"You are supposed to be some sort of master strategist. I think perhaps we have overestimated you all these years."

"Okay fellas," Mason says as he addresses the Legion members in his most authoritative tone. "As your unquestioned leader, I am commanding you to arrest Schmidt."

None say anything, instead keeping their weapons trained on him, closing in from all directions. Of course, Mason knew that would be the response, but he did it anyhow, just to buy a little time and encourage them to close in on him.

"Seriously. This is your last chance," Mason says.

"Come now, Mason. Even you can see when you are beaten."

All are well aware of how lethal Mason is and none of them take their eyes off him for one second. Armed with only a pistol, Mason knows that it will do little good in this situation, so he slowly uses two fingers to remove it from its holster and drops it to the floor and kicks it away, a calculated move. The other members of the Legion holster their weapons and await instruction like mindless robots.

"I'm glad you chose not to engage us," Schmidt says as he clasps his hands behind his back and begins strolling through the facility.

"Seemed kind of pointless, don't you think?"

"Yes, it would've been an exercise in futility," he says with an almost bored yawn that is meant to convey to Mason that he is now and has always been in complete control. "We really didn't want gunfire in here with all this sensitive equipment."

"Do you see these rockets? Do you know what they're for?" Mason asks.

"Yes. To fix the planet. Tod said you might try to get down here to disrupt that."

"Are you that dumb?"

"Watch your mouth grunt!" Schmidt chastises. "What I can't understand is why. Why would you want to delay the council's plans?"

"Tod is not what you think. Not what any of you think. He's evil. He's ..."

"Exactly what he said you'd say."

"Listen to me. Those rockets are going to destroy what's left of the Earth. To ruin it forever."

"Tod told me you'd say that, too," Schmidt says.

"It's true! Don't you see? You can't be that stupid."

"What I know, Mason, is that you are the only member of the Legion who regularly disobeys orders. The council is sick of it and frankly, so I am I."

"So now what?" Mason asks, crossing his arms across his chest in a defiant gesture that elicits a chuckle from Schmidt.

"Now? Now, you get to show your team members just how good you are."

Mason looks around the room, seeing the serious faces of five Legion members who have always been loyal to Schmidt. Each pull their blades and form a circle around Mason, who was the leader only because of his prowess, but have been clearly poisoned by Schmidt to be portrayed as a traitor. With a knife of his own, he could take any one of them, and likely even two, and they all know it. But all five is a death sentence.

"If you don't resist, I will make it quick," Schmidt offers, running his finger across the blade of his own knife with the cocky smirk of a man who holds all the cards. "Yield and we will slit your throat quick and easy, humane like putting down an animal.

"Go to hell," Mason shouts.

"That's what I hoped you'd say," Schmidt says. "So, it's the hard way then."

“I’m going to give you all one chance to live. Drop your weapons and surrender,” Mason orders. “Your only other option is going to be agonizing death.”

The Legion members eyeball Schmidt who has always hated the way Mason disobeyed him, bringing in half-breeds and allowing those on the outside to live when his instructions were clear. Even now, the Legion members pause, having never known Mason to be defeated in any situation.

Schmidt hates how he never truly bought into the purification cause. He always thought he was somehow above the rules. That he was special. It’s the most egregious behavior that any commanding officer worth his stripes must stomp out. Something he has been unable to do when dealing with Mason. So, this is personal.

“Prepare to die, Mason.”

“You first!”

“Kill him now!” Schmidt shrieks, his anger now at a fevered pitch.

The five men obey, charging Mason, who waits until they are almost on top of him, then he produces two, small, glass vials, dropping to a knee, smashing both containers onto the concrete floor. Immediately the liquid activates, a furious, pink gas billowing from the ground. The Legion members immediately drop their knives and grab their throats, beginning to froth at the mouth, falling to the ground in agony. Schmidt, standing more than 10 meters away, sees the danger and makes a run for the far door. But Mason pounces from his crouched position, removing his own knife from its sheath and throws it at Schmidt, hitting him in the upper back of the left leg, spearing his hamstring, dropping him to the ground. Mason quickly turns to Trevor, who is convulsing on the floor and pulls his handgun from its holster. He then slowly emerges from the poisonous smoke, walking deliberately toward Schmidt, who is laying on the floor.

"Reach for your firearm," Mason says, knowing that Schmidt doesn't have the courage to die like a true warrior.

"Wait. Mason, no," he pleads.

"Pull your gun!"

"No!" Schmidt shrieks.

Mason glances back at the five Legion members who are now in their death throes, spasming in agony. Mason considers dragging Schmidt over to where he can get a good whiff of the poison. With a shaky hand, the coward gently lifts his sidearm from its holster and slides it away.

"You can't even die like a man," Mason barks.

Schmidt, who has never seen combat, has the spooked eyes of a child. Just another of a long line of people in the Ark who never earned their position, but had it bestowed upon them because of their race and family.

Schmidt is confused for a moment, looking up at Mason as the chilling reality sets in that this ends in one of two ways.

"What was that?" Schmidt asks with confused eyes as he nods toward the now dead Legion.

"A particularly nasty version of Sarin."

"Sarin. But you. You were in it too."

"I was."

"What do you mean? How?"

"A parting gift from Ben."

"What?"

"I'm immune."

"That's impossible. Ben said when he tried, the subjects couldn't tolerate it."

"It's true. They could not."

During this conversation, while trying to look unassuming, Schmidt begins to try to stand up. Since Mason is the one man who doesn't kill in cold blood, he believes he can distract him with rhetoric.

"I was just following orders. That is all."

"Like a mindless puppet," Mason chastises, demonstratively holstering the weapon he took from Trevor. "That's all you have ever been. A coward hiding behind a desk, playing soldier but not having the guts to actually fight."

"Maybe you are right. Maybe I could learn from you," Schmidt says as he slowly makes his way to one knee, a clumsy move that nearly makes Mason laugh. Perhaps Schmidt has a speck of courage after all. Then in one, quick movement, Schmidt pulls the Derringer pistol from the concealed holster at the small of his back. He tries to aim it at Mason but is met with a furious right hand to the throat, crushing his thorax. He never even gets a shot off, falling to his back, his eyes wild with fear as his crushed windpipe is one of the worst ways to go.

"You can die like you lived. A helpless fraud," Mason says as he stands over his helpless foe.

Schmidt's mouth gapes like a fish pulled from the water, desperately trying to suck in air. Schmidt gasps, looking up in fear. Mason looks on in disgust at this man who needed to die hard. Mason gets a feeling of satisfaction as he watches Schmidt suffer, having enough time to realize what is happening, terror in his eyes. It takes him nearly a minute to finally stop struggling as his face glazes over.

AUDIO 8:

When Tod was first born, or created, he seemed to be an utter failure from a medical point of view. While the vital signs were all fine, the infant did nothing. While we could find no medical reason for it, the child did not respond to anything. He never cried, never smiled, never even moved. He was like that for the first 19 months.

He was kept alive through a feeding tube and other than urinating and defecating spontaneously, he did nothing else.

But one day that all changed. It was like a switch went off and suddenly he was full of life, rolling over, babbling like a child should and even smiling. We had no explanation for why he was so delayed, but it was a very exciting time.

From that point on, he learned at an exponential rate, and we were all so very hopeful that the prophecy was coming to fruition.

But soon, the child would become lethargic and then would go back to a lifeless husk. Then, in 10 to 15 hours, he would spring back to life, again flourishing before the same decline would happen again. It went on like this for quite a while.

We ran every test we could and finally discovered through blood tests that he was suffering from a condition we had never seen before as his body was destroying its own blood cells at an accelerated rate. Blood transfusions made matters worse, only hastening the process. I spent hour after hour, day after day by his side, pouring through blood samples, looking for answers. In a desperate attempt to save this life that we had created, I stumbled upon something never tried before.

Iron chelation is the process of removing iron from the body of a person who has too much. I know that doesn't mean anything to you, but it will to Rachel and other than you, she is the only person I trust here. You can and need to trust her, too.

Even though the iron levels in the transfusions were well within the normal parameters, we were desperate, so I decided to do iron chelation to the blood before transfusion. Basically, it means we removed all iron from the blood and then gave it to the subject. To our elation, the process worked. As it turns out, the subject who was later named Tod, a first name he chose, is severely allergic to iron. It's a condition I had never even heard of. We assumed that somewhere in the cloning process there was a genetic misstep or malformation that caused this. We incorrectly assumed that at 19 months he developed this iron allergy. A foolish assumption because that's also the time that he began to respond.

The blood transfusions were successful, and his body began working normally, but since his blood is void of iron it also depletes itself quickly, making weekly transfusions necessary since that day.

Tod's diet has also been created specifically for him. Before each meal, he takes a specially created powder called polyphenols, which block the absorption of even the smallest traces of iron. He then must adhere to a strict iron-free diet. That means most meats, many vegetables like asparagus, prunes, or beets, and even oatmeal will make him very ill. In fact, he is so allergic to iron that if he touches an iron door handle or tool, it immediately will scald his skin.

Like any good scientist, all I looked at were the test results, not considering anything not rooted in science. Tangible data was my only guiding force. Only recently did I consider other variables. That was the biggest mistake of my life. One that has cost this world everything.

CHAPTER FORTY-ONE

Upon dispatching the attacking members of the Legion, Mason met up with Rachel and Clark as planned and began searching for the council. Without the Legion, resistance should be minimal, and he is going to end this once and for all. Time is now of the essence. With Schmidt and his loyal band of brainwashed Legion members now dead, it won't take long for the council members to learn of this uprising. With so many secrets in the Ark, the last thing he wants is for them to escape to some hidden corridor where they can hole up like rodents.

Now having secured most of the security protocols necessary, they are able to break into the suites, an area Mason had never been to. Fortunately, Conrad was distracted and therefore was unaware of what was going on. He was too busy preparing to feed his depraved urges.

Upon finding Conrad's suite, Mason uses his thick, combat boot and kicks the door in, causing a startled Conrad, who is in a blue, silk robe to shriek.

"Hello sir!" Mason says. "I was worried you were in trouble and wanted to check on you."

The arrogant prick actually smiles wryly and asks in a condescending tone, "Mason. Are you supposed to be in this area?"

The smarmy look on his face is immediately removed by a powerful, open-handed slap to the side of Conrad's jaw that sends him sprawling to the floor, a high-pitched cry escaping his lips. Immediately Conrad begins whimpering and begging as this is surely the first time in his life that he has ever had anything mean done to him. Mason wants to break both of his legs, but he doesn't have the time for that right now. So instead, he hoists the scrawny man off the ground, slamming him against the wall and telling him he is about to die. The blubbering display is so off-putting that Mason must restrain himself from knocking him unconscious since he needs information.

The result was as he expected. Conrad instantly goes into self-preservation mode, answering any and all questions through convulsive sobs. Mason learns that Stephan is in a hidden corridor where he keeps young boys that he likes to visit. At first, he claimed not to know exactly where it is, but Mason helped him remember by breaking Conrad's thumb.

Dragging Conrad with him, Mason quickly finds this hidden corridor that is basically small, clean cells that house more than a dozen young boys and girls. The look on his face is pure horror when Mason enters the corridor to find Stephan looking over the children in the cells. Mason's rage takes over as he smashes Stephan's leg with a front kick that shatters his femur.

As Stephan tumbles to the floor, howling in agony, Mason has every intention of breaking his neck, but Rachel calmly grasps him by the shoulder and says, "No. That's the easy way out for him."

Realizing that she is right, he instead drags Stephan into an adjoining cell, shoving him in and locking him up right next to Conrad. Getting the keys from Stephan, they quickly unlock all of the cells where Rachel briefly explains the situation to the children, guiding them out of the corridor and into Conrad's suite. He will never be using it again. They are instructed to wait together with the promise of their freedom.

Now, it's Tod's turn. But Mason suspects that unlike his weakling council mates, Tod is probably aware of what is happening and has likely already taken action to escape or at least defend himself. Mason has considered the options and potential outcomes, trying to calculate the best course of action.

Conrad, a truly gutless individual with a perpetual weak constitution, needed little prodding to tell them where Tod's quarters are located, even giving them the code to get into the level where he resides. In a matter of minutes, Mason, Clark and Rachel navigate some narrow passageways to find the room.

Fully prepared to kick the door in, Mason is surprised when he reaches the room and sees the door ajar. He turns and eyeballs Clark and Rachel for a moment, the hackles on his neck rising as he can almost taste the danger. Somebody as cunning as Tod will not be taken easily and he likely has an entire arsenal at his disposal.

Finally, after a moment of hesitation, he gently pushes the heavy, wooden door, it swinging open with an eerie creak. The lights are off and a single candle is lit on the desk, offering the only illumination. Cautiously, with his firearm leading the way, Mason, while ducking low and moving deliberately, enters the space and to his surprise, Tod is sitting in a chair in the corner of the room, wearing leather gloves, brandishing a glimmering blade that he has pressed firmly against a trembling Lydia's throat.

Lydia? How? The air seemingly is sucked from the room as the others follow Mason into the room.

Clark drops to his knees when he sees her, a combination of relief and terror gripping him. How is she alive? Tod holds her up in front of him, using the small girl as a shield. Mason's instinct is to draw his gun and blow Tod's head clean off. But he knows that if he does, he will surely kill Lydia, and from what he has learned from Ben, probably won't kill Tod. To end all of this, he knows what he has to do. He pulls the gun, leveling it at Tod, whose head and torso is blocked by the child. Tod digs the knife into Lydia's neck, forcing her to cry out as blood trickles down her neck.

"Mason, no! Please!" Clark begs.

"He must die." Mason says evenly, playing his part to perfection.

"Mason, wait!" Rachel pleads.

"He needs to die," Mason says, putting his acting skills on full display, even forcing his gun hand to tremble a bit.

"No. Don't. You can't. She will die, too," Clark pleads.

Tod says nothing, instead watching intently, a hint of a smile on his face. While he doesn't wish to be shot, he knows he won't die. He has a contingency plan that will ensure that he never floats around aimlessly again. But still, he'd rather not have to go through all of that just yet.

Finally, after more than a minute in this standoff, Mason drops the gun to the ground.

"If you'd be so kind, move over there," Tod says, pointing to the wall where the decorative blanket with the Nazi logo that adorned that wall is down, revealing four sets of shackles that are bolted to the wall.

The trio slowly obey, stopping in front of the chains.

"Rachel, if you'd be so kind," Tod says, now peeking out from behind his human shield, the blade still digging into her neck.

Rachel does as she is instructed, first shackling Mason's arms to the wall, followed by doing the same to Clark. Tod could kill them both, but he feels that he needs an audience. In the end, he will cast them into der Kerker to suffer. But for now, he wants them here. He is reveling in his victory.

"Okay. We've done what you have asked, now let her go," Clark shouts. "Lydia, honey. It's going to be okay."

"No Lydia. It most certainly isn't going to be okay." Tod says, a raspy cough following his labored statement as this body is weakening.

"You don't look too good, Tod." Mason says with a sneer, seeing how Tod is obviously declining in health.

"Oh, I will be okay. That is, after Rachel and I make a trip to the infirmary. I'm a few days past due, but I've been preoccupied."

"Why would I help you?" she asks. "You're a monster."

He scoffs, and with some effort, gets up from the chair, still holding the blade to Lydia's neck.

For the past few sessions since Ben's death, a nurse has been helping with his transfusions, but soon most of these people will no longer be walking around free. For that reason, he has decided that Rachel will do the job until further notice.

Tod moves across the floor, bending over and picking up the gun, then throwing Lydia to the ground and aiming the firearm at Rachel. She bristles at him, lifting her chin in defiance, causing a smile from Tod. He then slowly moves the gun to Lydia.

"No. Please. If you must shoot somebody, shoot me," Clark pleads.

Tod grins, obliging Clark and aiming the gun at him. Clark closes his eyes, bracing himself for the shot. Clark's whole body jerks as the deafening sound of the echoing gunshot elicits shocked screams from Rachel and Lydia. Clark slowly opens his eyes and looks down at his body, very surprised. At the last second, Tod moved the gun and shot Mason in the leg, causing skin and blood to splatter the wall. Tod looks on with a hint of a smile but Mason won't even give him the satisfaction of crying out in pain. Instead, he just stares at Tod, a burning hate in his eyes. Mason now wishes he had shot Tod when he had the chance.

"You really are tough," Tod says. "A soldier right up to the end."

Tod walks over, quickly examining the shackles on the wrists and ankles of Clark and Mason. Tod even takes the end of the gun and pushes it into the wound, the sickening sound of burnt flesh and muscle squeezing together, causing more bleeding. Mason could kick at him, possibly breaking his leg or arm. But he chooses not to react, having been shot before, he knows it's just a flesh wound. He will heal as he always does. Mason does have the urge to spit in Tod's face but won't give him the satisfaction of knowing how powerless he feels. Tod then turns back to Rachel, walks across the room, his breathing labored, before grabbing Lydia by the hair and dragging her to her feet.

"How is Lydia still alive?" Clarks asks. "I checked her vitals myself."

"Just a little compound to slow respiration for a while. As you can see, she's no worse for wear."

"Why?"

"It was Conrad's doing to be quite honest. In a few years, she was to be another one of his sex slaves I imagine. Disgusting animals that you all are, guided by your groins. But, as it turns out, she also turned out to be a pretty good bargaining chip in case something unexpected happened. Since you are all here, I can safely assume that the Legion failed to deactivate you, Mason."

Tod then turns back to Rachel, now looking very tired.

"So? Shall we?" Tod says with a motion toward the door, indicating that they are going to the small infirmary on this level where his treatments take place.

After a moment of trepidation, Rachel exits the room, with Tod following as he drags Lydia along, just in case Rachel needs some motivation.

CHAPTER FORTY-TWO

Rachel clicks on the light, illuminating the utilitarian space that features white, tile walls and stainless-steel equipment. Tod follows, still brandishing the gun and dragging Lydia by the back of the neck. Tod is out of breath and desperately in need of the procedure. He is dizzy from the short walk and has to shake his head a few times to keep this weak body alert.

After standing motionless for a moment, unwilling to help administer Tod's treatment, Tod sighs demonstratively, pulling Lydia hard by the hair, eliciting a frightened yelp from the little girl, pressing the gun hard against her face.

"Rachel. Are you going to cooperate, or do I need to make an example of this girl to motivate you?"

After glaring at Tod for a moment, she realizes that she has no choice. Rachel goes to the refrigeration unit against the far wall, removing a package of blood, placing it on a steel table. Tod frowns at her, still huffing and puffing from the short walk. He shoves Lydia to the ground before moving over to a small, stainless steel, freestanding refrigerator. He stoops down and puts his eyes to the scanning nodule, causing the hatch to click, unlocking the latch on the storage container.

"Not that I don't trust you," Tod says about the unit that he is the only one with access to. "Use one of these instead."

Only Tod has the retinal scan to open the hatch where this blood is stored. For the time being, until he is certain that Rachel has been sufficiently motivated to do his bidding, Tod will opt to use one of the dozens of units that Ben prepared well before his death. Ultimately, Tod has enough knowledge to create his own blood packets, which he will have ample time to do once he is done with his plan.

Tod then sits down, rolling up his sleeve while Rachel angrily removes the blood and prepares it. Tod keeps the gun trained on Lydia who is at his feet, ensuring Rachel's compliance.

"Why so angry?"

"Because I hate you."

"And I you," Tod responds.

"Why? I've never done anything but obey orders."

"It's nothing personal. It's not just you. I hate all of you."

"All of us? But why?"

Tod laughs, genuinely amused because he truly loves to make these humans suffer. He gets actual joy from their misery. He muses about how stupid these humans are in their sentimentality. After all, he was armed with just a knife and an inconsequential little girl. They could have easily overpowered him if only they were willing to let Lydia die. But since he's become an expert in human behavior since he's been with them since the beginning, he knew that these people would sacrifice everything just to keep her alive. So stupid. No wonder it was so easy to plunge the world into chaos.

Rachel remains silent during the preparation of the blood, slamming the refrigeration doors shut and banging around the equipment.

"You should be happy. You are only one of a select few for whom life is going to be tolerable."

"Tolerable?"

"Sure. Other than you and a few others, all that will remain for everybody else is going to be misery and ultimately death. But you have value and will be needed. For that reason, you will be fed and clothed as long as you do your job."

"And what exactly is my job?" she asks defiantly.

"To do exactly what I tell you to do, when I tell you to do it."

"You're a monster."

"Yes. I am."

"You don't even deny it?"

"Why should I. I'm not embarrassed by whom I am."

"You mean by what you are?"

Tod laughs softly, not so much amused by the statement as he is about the fact that she clearly knows more than he thought.

"Rachel my dear, I'm as old as time itself, having existed since the beginning. I evolved over the years from a drifting consciousness into an all-knowing presence that has impacted and shaped this world since the earliest days of humanity."

"Pure evil."

"Hmmm. I never thought about it that way," Tod ponders her words for a moment. "Perhaps you are right. I wasn't always this way, though. For more millenniums than you can imagine, I enjoyed my time with humans. When you first discovered fire, I was there. I watched as you lived in caves, finally learning how to build shelters, watched as your gibberish transformed painfully slowly into language. I watched kingdoms grow and then be toppled, watched the Earth change and continents drift apart. I am essentially the biographer of human life."

"And now?"

"Now, I want all of you to suffer. I want nothing more than that. I want revenge on your people, as well as others like me. And yes, ultimately, I want you all to suffer miserably."

"You've gone mad."

"Yes. Perhaps I have," Tod says. "Centuries in isolation tend to sour a being."

"You know, your body won't last forever. Then what?"

"Oh my. I never thought about that," Tod says with a sarcastic tone. "Before Ben's untimely demise, he helped me ensure that I can live forever."

Rachel sighs, realizing that he is telling her about other cloned bodies. Angrily, she continues to prepare the transfusion, finally moving to Tod and setting up the I.V., hands shaking nervously as Tod turns the handgun on her.

"My dear, I am all-knowing. I'm the orchestrator of life and death. I am immortal!"

While not painful, Tod finds the procedure unpleasant, so as always, he tries to take his mind off it by thinking about something else. On this day, that means going into the past.

The earliest memories, if Tod can even call them memories, are of clanging around aimlessly in the Realm, one of countless specs of energy not unlike a bowl of tadpoles, simply existing. Eons passed and this remained unchanged, boring, but since this is all that ever was, none of them knew any better.

But one day, there was something else, something new. Just beyond the only home it ever knew, these life forces became aware of another place taking shape. A place they could only quantify as "somewhere else." Their instincts told them to explore it. As with anything else, it took a long time before even a few figured out how to escape.

Finally, they discovered that when a cluster of them teemed together and pressed with all of their effort, they could puncture the outer boundary of the Realm where they emerged into a strange world full of wonder. Immediately, they would scatter to all parts of what they learned was called a planet. Full of creatures both large and small, it was unlike anything they'd ever experienced before.

Almost like an addiction, after so long being stuck in what was essentially a fishbowl with nothing other than themselves, they had a new world, full of a variety of ever-changing life. It was intoxicating to them.

But the biggest discovery was yet to come. There was a powerful force in each being that beckoned to them. By accident at first, just by being inquisitive creatures, the first of them entered a human body and the rush of energy was unlike anything any of them had ever experienced before. Every molecule in the body of any human they entered became saturated with the energy of each entity. Suddenly, they were looking at the world through the actual eyes of these creatures. It was like nothing any of them had ever known. Through these surrogate hosts, these beings were able to experience actual tactile functions such as touching, tasting, hearing, seeing and much more.

Ultimately, all could only stay for a short while, as something about the bonding process would weaken each entity to the point where they would be eventually ripped from the host, drained of their energy, where they would be pulled back and re-emerge in the Realm to recharge before doing it again. These beings who had lived so long, unchanged, basically unthinking, existing mostly out of instinct, had suddenly evolved into something else. Soon they learned that bonding with these humans yielded an unexpected gift. Each time they left their human hosts, they retained all the knowledge that individual had. In almost no time at all, this entire race of energy-based beings had individual consciousness. Learning at an exponential rate, they absorbed knowledge about subjects more numerous than any could imagine. As these humans began to grow as a civilization, over the millenniums' that followed, the use of tools, language and culture grew and with it, so did the intellect of each of them.

While most of these beings were perfectly happy to just ride along and soak in all of the experiences, Tod, as he is called now, as well as a few others like him, discovered that they had the ability to actually cause change. Tod began to realize that with some effort, he could influence whatever human who it was riding in. At first, it was little things, like causing the person to rub his or her chin or run their fingers through their hair. But with practice, he began to be able to actually influence the human for a very, short period of time.

But Tod became ambitious and wanted to affect real change. And that's when the real fun began.

Over the centuries, as the human race grew, Tod helped orchestrate change, causing chaos along the way. The experience of having actual effect on this world was incredibly addictive. Others of Tod's kind disapproved of his actions, believing that this symbiotic relationship was a gift that should be cherished, and that this kind of treachery could ultimately harm this relationship. But none could do anything to stop Tod. So, while most of these creatures enjoyed a peaceful, non-intrusive union with these humans, Tod relished the opportunity to control what he deemed lesser beings. With the ability to see each other while in the physical world or when riding with a human, these beings, invisible to humans, were aware of Tod's actions. Therefore, when back in the Realm, which had also evolved into a community of sorts over the years, they shunned Tod and a few others who they deemed were breaking their laws, something they learned from the humans. For many centuries, the collective would no longer allow Tod and the others who broke this law to exit the Realm. It was simple to enforce. Since it takes a small Army of them working together to burst out of the Realm, they simply wouldn't help.

So that's how it was for a long time. Tod, now aware of Earth and its everchanging wonder, remained stuck. Rarely would Tod ever escape the Realm. The few times he did, it was only when he would sneak in at the tail end of a team push, riding through the rift. Being ostracized in this manner made Tod become bitter and angry. So now, in the rare times he did make it to

Earth, there was no more subtlety as he tried to unleash as much carnage as possible before eventually weakening and getting sucked back to the Realm.

But on his last trip to Earth, Tod happened upon a host who was different. He stumbled upon a teenage girl from a wealthy family with a medical condition that made her weak and tired often, but it also didn't drain him like the other human hosts he encountered. Weeks and weeks went by, him guiding her into one atrocity after another, yet he remained. It was a wonderful, fulfilling existence, one that had been torn away from Tod that fateful day when he was cast into exile by that religious fool, only able to look on while others like him came and went with ease. Every second of it was agonizing, with no relief for century after century.

Now, they will all pay.

CHAPTER FORTY-THREE

Tod almost immediately feels better, the color coming back into his cheeks as the transfusion revitalizes his body as usual. Now, walking back to his quarters, with Lydia and Rachel walking in front of him, Tod has a smile on his face. He feels invincible as his plan is now coming to fruition. He cannot wait to see their faces for what comes next. After all these years, finally he can end this charade. Finally, he can show them all that he is indeed all powerful. Most importantly, now he gets to have his revenge.

Having Rachel unshackle Clark and Mason, he instructs them to travel through a dizzying array of hallways, into an observation area that nobody else has access to. Even with a bullet wound, Mason manages to walk without a limp, a testament to just what kind of a warrior he is. Tod has seen more than his share of humans, but he has never seen anybody quite like Mason. If he didn't hate everybody so much, Tod thinks he could almost admire him.

Tod wonders why he feels it necessary to share his plan with them. It kind of bothers him because doing it is something akin to pride, which is a stupid, human emotion. After all, Mason and Lydia will be tossed into der Kerker as soon as the demonstration is over, and Clark and Rachel will be confined to cells since their medical knowledge will still be necessary. Perhaps all these years posing as a human has allowed some of their primal urges to manifest in himself.

But that is something he can sort out later because having an audience for his crowning moment is necessary. Perhaps it is because he needs a witness to record this moment. He likes the thought of that better than the need to have his ego stroked.

Tod opens the final latch, allowing the large, metal door to swing inward, before stepping away and ushering them into the space with a wave of the gun. They enter the space and after forcing them to sit where they have a good view of the hangar area, Tod moves across the long, thin room to the command area. He laughs audibly as he sees the dead Legion members scattered across the floor, as well as Commander Schmidt.

"Your work, Mason?" Tod says with a hint of a smile.

"I took no joy in killing them. Their blood is on your hands," Mason hisses.

"And you think that somehow that upsets me? They all served their purpose. I care about their deaths as much as a swatted insect."

"They were fools. And they followed the directions of a madman," Mason says.

"A madman? Try genius. But no matter. Call me what you will. You see, now we have reached the epic conclusion."

"Conclusion?" Rachel asks.

"Apparently, you know more about me than I guessed. But let me bring you up to speed," Tod says, as he begins moving his hands up and down his body in a demonstrative fashion. "These fools grew this body in a lab for the preposterous purpose of leading some purified race. It's laughable that these chosen people, Aryans, feel they are somehow better than any other. You all crawl around the ground, your grotesque forms doing nothing more than eating, defecating, and climbing on top of each other to satisfy your carnal lust. It's pathetic. I've watched the rise and fall of civilizations too numerous to recall. But you all had one thing in common. You are nothing more than mindless apes."

"You know, you are human too?" Clark quips.

"I most certainly am not," Tod shouts. "This is a mere tool. That is all. This is simply a vehicle for me, nothing more. The plan that I have executed in this last half century is one that I and I alone made happen. Everything that has occurred. The world we now live in. I am responsible."

"But you still needed humans. Without us creating this body that you despise, you are powerless," Rachel says with disgust in her voice.

"No!" Tod snaps, already angry that he has allowed these lesser-evolved beings to banter with him. "I am a God!"

"A God who needs a blood transfusion to stay alive," she says.

Tod feels feverish with anger and must resist the urge to put a bullet between her eyes. But even though he doesn't want to admit it, he does need her for his treatments. So instead, he forces a condescending smile at her, trying to showcase control that he feels slipping away.

Tod points to the hangar bay while pressing a few buttons on the control panel in front of him. Steel doors grind to life, each above the three rockets that have already been loaded into their delivery brackets and moved into place. After several moments they open completely to reveal cavernous tubes.

"You all should feel lucky," Tod says, his voice becoming raspy. "You four get to witness something special."

"What's that?" Clark asks. "A man's descent into madness?"

"You get to witness the end of the world, of course," Tod says in a matter-of-fact manner meant to convey just how meaningless he feels humans are.

"Pretty short-sighted, don't you think?" Mason says.

"How so?"

"Well, if you end the world, then what?"

"Then, the real fun begins."

"What? This plan of yours to destroy the world? Why?"

Tod stands quiet for a moment, pondering the question. Finally, since it doesn't really matter, he decides to tell them the truth.

"Revenge."

"Revenge?" Rachel says in disbelief. "All this because … somebody hurt your feelings. It's so pathetic that I almost feel bad for you."

Tod feels a pang of anger boiling under the surface.

"I can't expect your limited intellect to understand all of this," Tod tries to say evenly but it coming out in an agitated bark.

"Look at you, standing there trying to sound like some kind of omnipotent being," Mason chastises with a mocking laugh that is meant to belittle Tod. "The same guy who held a knife to the throat of a little girl."

"Enough of this," Tod shouts, his anger taking over as he begins punching buttons on the control panel, springing a wall of lights and gauges to life while the hangar beyond the protective, glass wall begins to hum with the sound of the rockets being activated.

Tod refuses to waste any more time. He has waited long enough for vindication. First this, then the members of the Ark will be herded to der Kerker. That will be simple enough to accomplish as he will systematically shut off life support to areas of the Ark. They will be instructed by the speakers throughout the facility to go to der Kerker, the only place with oxygen. Their only option will be to go to der Kerker voluntarily, sliding through the chute, or suffocate. Tod doesn't care either way.

Steam and rumbling begin to emit from the hangar as the rockets vibrate to life, the pre-launch sequence preparing for liftoff. Tod now has everything he needs to exact revenge on everybody and everything for his centuries of suffering.

"I wasn't planning for everything to happen so quickly. But when I discovered that you three were becoming aware of the plan, I had to move things up a bit. But it doesn't matter. I've planned for every contingency."

"So now what?" Mason says. "You're going to launch missiles out there? What for? Everything is already destroyed."

"Not everything. Not yet. But very soon," Tod says, pointing a shaky finger toward the hangar and then flipping open a plastic cover and then turning a large, metal key.

The first of the three rockets lift off, the hangar filling with superheated steam that vaporizes Schmidt's body, left right where Mason killed him. The rocket vibrates the entire observation deck with such ferocity that Lydia cries out, covering her ears with her hands.

Tod smiles triumphantly, raising his arms in victory and laughing. He then follows the same procedure two more times.

The other two rockets follow suit, rumbling through the previously hidden missile silos. Tod laughs from the safety of the observation deck as the sound of the rockets slowly fade away as they are preprogrammed, and nothing can stop them from reaching their destinations. When each reaches their designated locations, the Earth will cease to exist.

"In a matter of weeks, a month at the most, the Earth will no longer be able to sustain any life," Tod says proudly. "And you had the privilege of seeing it. You got to witness the end of the world."

"Let me guess, you're going to kill all of us next, and everybody in the Ark?" Clark asks with a hint of defiance in his voice.

"Oh no. That is definitely not the plan. Everybody in here will hopefully live long, miserable lives," Tod says, wiping some sweat from his forehead. "I alone am responsible for the end of this world. You remaining few will spend the rest of your lives in der Kerker. Other than breeding, which you will do, you will serve no other purpose."

"What is der Kerker?" Mason asks.

"You will find out very soon," Tod says with a hoarse whisper.

"But why?" Rachel asks.

“So, I can watch you all suffer, of course. Suffer like I have for century after century,” Tod says with a cough that tastes somewhat metallic.

“So that’s it,” Mason inquires. “Your only goal is to create suffering. You’re pathetic.”

“You won’t think that after a few years in der Kerker,” Tod says, breaking into a violent, coughing fit, finally bringing up some bloody phlegm.

“What’s the matter?” Rachel asks with a caring tone that is dripping is sarcasm.

Tod is now keenly aware that something is very wrong. His eyes begin to water uncontrollably and as he wipes them, he discovers there is actually blood leaking from around his eye sockets.

“What have you done?” Tod demands, now falling against the wall, sliding to the floor, a burning sensation beginning inside his bones.

“What do you mean?” she asks.

“Answer me. What did you do to me?” he tries to scream, but his words come out in an agonizing whisper.

“I gave you the transfusion as you commanded,” Rachel sings in a melodious tone. “From the locked vault you asked for. If you remember, I tried to give you different blood, but you were just so insistent.”

“How?” he gurgles as his mouth begins to fill with blood.

“Ben.”

“Ben?” Tod mouths.

“From the grave, Ben told Mason what you are,” Rachel says with a disgusted snort. “About the monster he helped create.”

“You treacherous whore! You’ve poisoned me. You will pay for this. Pay dearly.”

“I had help,” Rachel says, pointing to Clark.

An expert in blood, Clark used what he was told about Tod's iron allergy to create blood packets that were packed full of a specially synthesized protein called ferritin. Ferritin stores iron, only releasing it when iron levels in the blood are low. Clark theorized that these mega doses of ferritin in the blood transfusion would be unrecognized when administered but would go to work when the protein recognized the absence of any iron. Whether it would happen immediately, or in hours was anyone's guess. Clark believed the iron would slowly overwhelm Tod, making him very weak. But what actually occurred was unexpectedly quick.

Tod desperately tries to raise the gun but is already too weak as blood has begun to trickle out of his ears, his skin producing bubbling boils before their eyes. Mason gets up, walks over and kicks the gun away from him.

Tod's eyes begin to sink into his skull and his skin has begun to liquefy, causing him to howl in pain, gasping but still trying to speak.

"You'll all die," he slurs through bloody spittle. "You'll live underground like rodents until your supplies run out and you'll all die."

"Oh. You mean those rockets?" Mason says as he points to the sky, having already removed the canisters of Reinigen. "Those rockets will go where you want them to go. But without your precious poison."

Tod lets out a scream, part pain, part in the knowledge that he has failed and is about to be relieved from this body. His bubbling form then bursts into flames as his energy that animates this cloned body is ignited by the iron, the body dissolving into a gelatinous puddle.

Suddenly there is no physical pain, but something much worse. Tod drifts above the room, seeing these primates that somehow defeated him scurrying around the observation deck, hugging each other. Making matters worse is the fact that each of them have beings riding along too. They are also celebrating with jubilance at the defeat. Tod tries to scream, but there is no sound. Relegated to being an observer again, could there be anything worse?

Tod is furious with these fools. Don't they know that Tod has planned for every scenario, his intellect far superior to any who have ever been. Their suffering will be more severe than anything they can imagine.

Tod immediately phases through the rock wall, navigating to a hidden chamber that houses the matured clone that is existing in a coma-like state in an environmental tube. This one was to be used if Tod's body were to become injured or breakdown. Tod wiggles through the opening at the base of the tube to animate the clone, this one younger, just 22 years in age. Tod enters the body and almost immediately, this body that hasn't done anything for more than two decades, begins to move. But there is something wrong. Tod can't see. With some effort, he brings a shaky hand up to feel his face and realizes there are two patches where his eyes should be.

Gibby, one of the Legion members that Mason knows he can trust, followed his orders perfectly. Stationed in a dark corner of the room where he could watch the body of Tod's replacement clone, the moment he sees it move, he quickly jumps into action.

The second Tod touches the patched eyes, he realizes that it is a trap. Clearly the eyes were removed so that Rachel could use them to get into the vault and tamper with his blood. Tod immediately tries to flee, but he hears the hatch slam shut and Tod's chilling reality is that there is indeed something worse than being an observer. Desperately he exits the body and tries to phase through the tube but is immediately thrown back violently. This iron-lined interior has imprisoned Tod. When Ben created the tube to house this clone, he secretly fortified it with iron so if needed, Tod could be captured. The trap worked to perfection. Now there is nothing. Tod is left with nothing but his own consciousness, alert in inky blackness, and nothing else, forever. It tries to scream out but can't. This will be its eternal existence.

AUDIO 9:

Ultimately, I now know that Tod's iron weakness has nothing to do with his human biology. My research has come to just one possible conclusion. He wasn't allergic to iron for the first year and a half. That issue only came about when he started to respond. I now believe that when this entity that became Tod entered the empty vessel I helped create, it's the non-human side that courses through that body that cannot tolerate iron. Basically, the iron in the blood is constantly trying to reject its host.

Always a man of science and science alone, only when I explored other scenarios did I learn about possibilities that I once dismissed as make believe. History is peppered with tales of beings of evil origins who were seemingly invulnerable yet couldn't tolerate iron. Iron shackles and weapons were used to vanquish these beings who have had countless names over the years. As it turns out, those beings were Tod and I suspect a few others like him, or it. These beings are basically allergic to iron.

I'm ashamed that only now am I coming to this conclusion.

I used to believe in pushing the boundaries of science into any arena, but I now know that some things are not meant for man to meddle in. When I helped create Tod, a name he chose when he reached his teens and which means death in ancient German, I created the first being to be born without a soul. In doing so, I opened the door to allow something terrible into this world. I created the perfect conduit for evil to live and thrive.

Tod orchestrated the end of our civilization as we know it. But I am just as responsible as he or it. I have been a fool. A stupid, small-minded man with a misguided agenda that has ruined what was once a beautiful, albeit flawed, world.

Mason, my hope is that you will be able to stop him. That you can somehow salvage this world. You have always been special to me. In fact, more special than even you know. I am heartbroken at the path you were forced to travel. But I am so proud of you because through it all, you have become a strong and decent person. There has never been anybody like you. Now I need to finally tell you about your origins. You were not an orphan. In fact, your father always knew exactly where you were at all times. It had to be that way if you were to be chosen. You are not of pure blood, which is why I falsified all of your tests. While your father was of a pure, Aryan bloodline, your mother was not. Even though your father was always loyal to the cause of purity, the heart wants what the heart wants.

When your father fell in love with your mother, it was in secret. And when you arrived, your true lineage was concealed. When the end was upon us, at your mother's begging, your father arranged for you to be chosen. I arranged it. You see son, I am your father. I wanted to tell you a million times, but I couldn't risk you being found out. My heart broke when you and the other orphans were tested for possible inclusion in the Legion. Each time you scored higher than everybody else, it sealed your fate in this life. So even though you never knew it, your father has always been with you, secretly trying to guide you as best I could. That is why I recorded this message for you so that in the event that I am gone, the recharging of your implants without my specific code would trigger the message.

Now you have work to do. Use this knowledge to vanquish Tod. Use those few around you that you can trust to help you. I'm not sure if Tod can be killed, but he can be trapped. Of that I am certain. You can help create a new and better tomorrow. You can rebuild this fractured world that I unknowingly helped destroy.

I believe in you. Others will too. Lead them, Mason. Lead them my son!

CHAPTER FORTY-FOUR

With the corrupt Legion members and their commander out of the way, Mason gets Rachel, Clark and Gibby and they begin tending to the children removed from the cells that Conrad and Stephan kept them in. During interrogation, it takes almost no pressure at all and each turns on the other one. During the session, Conrad lets it slip about how der Kerker wasn't his idea, that it was Tod's. Upon hearing the horror of this hidden dungeon, Gibby immediately wants to kill them, but Mason has no more desire for loss of life. Instead, he opts to imprison them for the rest of their lives. It's better than they deserve, but it's an important step in re-establishing values in the Ark.

With the prevailing government of the Ark now no longer in power, Mason is able to move through the facility unimpeded.

Since der Kerker is essentially a pit that people are dropped into, Mason, Gibby and a couple other recruits he trusts use sledgehammers to break through a wall on the ground level. When they eventually punch through, Mason steps through first and even he cannot believe the hell that these people have been living in. He steps inside, followed by Rachel and Clark. Rachel and Clark are in biohazard gear, something Mason does not need. The living conditions are worse than anything Mason could have ever imagined.

Vance is the first to approach them, as the others are afraid, unsure what fresh hell is about to be unleashed upon them. Even though he has only been there a short time, the plight of this place is clear.

"Are? Are you here to kill us or help us?" Vance asks, his face telling Mason that either would be preferrable to staying in this hellacious prison.

The dark dungeon becomes quiet as the suffering inhabitants of der Kerker look on, having never seen anybody other than new prisoners enter.

"My name is Mason. We are here to free you," he says, his words echoing through the chamber.

Slowly at first, but then growing into an all-encompassing cheer, the space erupts with jubilation by all who are still alive.

For some reason, Mason knows exactly what to say, even though he has never delivered a speech in his life. Mason addresses them all in a confident and powerful voice, telling everybody in the dungeon who he is, where they are and that they are being freed and that this nightmare is over.

With the leadership of the Ark in question, people naturally gravitate toward Mason. While never viewing himself as a leader, Mason does have all the qualities. Now knowing where he comes from and his place in this world thanks to Ben, his father, Mason is up to the task. He immediately begins working on a plan to transform the Ark so that the influx of new members can be cared for.

Within a matter of weeks, the people of the Ark, now with all the facts about this place, follow their new leader without question.

After exhausting all medical personnel in an effort to restore the health of the former residents of der Kerker, when ready, the new members are integrated into the community. For the younger members, the transition was easier, but breaking down the barriers of bigotry in many of the older members took some time. Some will likely never get completely over the engrained feelings of superiority that a lifetime of brainwashing caused. But that doesn't matter. In the end, everybody will choose to believe what they want, just as it has always been.

It took some planning, including remodeling many of the living quarters, including transforming the suites into apartments, and changing how supplies will be rationed, but the Ark will adjust to its new normal.

The corridors, hatch and broken wall to der Kerker is sealed off, never to be seen again. But before that is done, the tube containing Tod is placed in a secondary, square, iron-like coffin constructed by the Ark's blacksmith and apprentice per Mason's specifications to ensure that Tod cannot ever escape and is placed in der Kerker where it can suffer for all eternity inside the iron tube with the slowly decaying, dead body. Additionally, the frozen embryos of the man once known as Adolf Hitler are all destroyed so such a calamity can never again be duplicated.

All of them look to Mason for leadership, a man who was bred to be a killer, but ended up being a savior.

With every race now intermingling in this underground sanctuary, they are now waiting for the skies to one day clear so they can re-emerge. It will be a long time before that day arrives and is unclear if anybody will still be alive up top when that day comes, but they have all the tools necessary to restart this world. Will they learn from their past mistakes? Will they rebuild our world, free of corruption and evil? Will coming so close to extinction give them wisdom? That will remain to be seen. But one thing is for sure. These few remaining humans will have the herculean task of restarting the Earth.

ABOUT THE AUTHOR

David McElhinny is a longtime writer, editor and columnist from Pennsylvania. He lives in a town called Mars, with his wife, Bonnie, and two children, Sean and Adam.

ABOUT THE PUBLISHER

Creative Texts is a boutique independent publishing house devoted to high quality content that readers enjoy. We publish best-selling authors such as C.W. Wells, Jerry D. Young, N.C. Reed, Sean Liscom, Jared McVay, Laurence Dahners, and many more. Our audiobook performers are among the best in the business including Hollywood legends like Barry Corbin and top talent like Christopher Lane, Alyssa Bresnaham, Erin Moon and Graham Hallstead.

Whether its post-apocalyptic or dystopian fiction, biography, history, true crime science fiction, thrillers, or even classic westerns, our goal is to produce highly rated customer preferred content. If there is anything we can do to enhance your reader experience, please contact us directly at info@creativetexts.com. As always, we do appreciate your reviews on your book seller's website.

Finally, if you would like to find more great books like this one, please search for us by name in your favorite search engine or on your bookseller's website to see books by all Creative Texts authors. Thank you for reading!

www.ingramcontent.com/pod-product-compliance
Lightning Source LLC
LaVergne TN
LVHW010613100826
845148LV00014B/2943
* 9 7 8 1 6 4 7 3 8 0 7 8 6 *